"Is your affair with her over now, Nick?"

All Claudia's pent-up anger burst from her. "Is it? Do you want forgiveness?"

"From *you*?" He caught her wrists, and her heart pulsed in her throat. "Who are you to forgive me anything? Grant Ingram's spoiled-rotten angel. What experience have you of life to judge anyone?"

Claudia laughed harshly. "Oh no, Nick. You're not going to get out of it that way. There are penalties one pays for taking another man's wife. For taking my father's wife!"

"What about his daughter?"

"She hates you."

"I don't mind." His handsome face was drawn into an austere mask.

"Don't touch me, Nick," she warned.

"Because you couldn't bear it," he drawled, "or because you really want it?"

Books by Margaret Way

HARLEQUIN ROMANCES

HARLEQUIN PRESENTS

These books may be available at your local bookseller.

Don't miss any of our special offers. Write to us at the following address for information on our newest releases.

Harlequin Reader Service
P.O. Box 52040, Phoenix, AZ 85072-2040
Canadian address: P.O. Box 2800, Postal Station A,
5170 Yonge St., Willowdale, Ont. M2N 6J3

Fallen Idol

Margaret Way

Harlequin Books

TORONTO • NEW YORK • LONDON
AMSTERDAM • PARIS • SYDNEY • HAMBURG
STOCKHOLM • ATHENS • TOKYO • MILAN

Original hardcover edition published in 1984
by Mills & Boon Limited

ISBN 0-373-02700-1

Harlequin Romance first edition June 1985

CHAPTER ONE

IT was the night of her twenty-first birthday party and Claudia stood by the balustrade looking down at the floodlit garden. It was springtime and the terraces were aflame with colour; great drifts of azaleas, hundreds of them, running right down the hillside to the river; a vast sweep of velvety, green lawn and the boundaries of their large property bordered by jacarandas, exquisite in their flowering. Hundreds of camellias had been stripped from the bushes to float across the jewelled surface of the swimming pool, a glorious variety of shapes and colours. She wore white camellias in her hair, one perfect bloom behind each ear. She was a true platinum blonde and for tonight her long hair had been drawn back off her face and arranged in shining, intricate coils at her nape. It was her own idea to use the camellias. They were her favourite flowers and if they looked marvellous in her hair, she didn't seem to care.

In a short while the first of their guesets would be arriving. Her father had hired people to take care of the parking. Two hundred invitations had gone out. She could see Fergy making a last minute inspection of the big striped marquee that had been erected to the right of the pool area. This was to serve as an additional bar and buffet area and the entrance had been flanked by two enormous brass bound timber planters bearing

magnificent clusters of the rhododendron
Cleopatra in a brilliant red.

It should be one of the happiest nights of her
life, but Claudia's happiness had been shattered
months ago. Then she had discovered Cristina,
her stepmother, was having an affair with Nick.
Of course they had denied it vehemently. Nick,
especially, had been furiously angry. He had even
slapped her and she wouldn't forget *that* either as
long as she lived.

Dominic Grey

Her father's protégé. The brilliant young
architect who had been accepted straight out of
university into one of the most prestigious
architectural firms in the country. Nick's was a
great success story. Her father often said Nick
had been born knowing more than most architects
could squeeze into a lifetime's practise. He had
been so impressed with Nick he had taken him on
as his personal assistant. Now after seven years,
Nick was a full partner and a legend on his own.

Legends. Legends and idols. Ever since she
had first met him at the tender, terribly
impressionable age of thirteen, Claudia had
idolised Nick. He was so much more than a
highly gifted young man. He was remarkable in
so many ways. There was a tremendous vitality,
awareness, a certainty in him that her father called
the certainty of natural genius. Nick was only a
young man yet men like her father, at the very
top of their profession listened to him when he
spoke; took his drawings into their hands with the
kind of attention only given to a master, rarely an
apprentice.

Damn you, Nick!

Once when she and her father had been sitting quietly together he had told her Nick was the son he had always longed for ... 'Understand, darling, you're as perfect a daughter as I could ever wish for, but *Nick*! You'll have to grow up quickly and marry him, my angel!' her father had joked. A joke, yet *not* a joke and Claudia had laughed sadly. She knew what Nick meant to her father. She had seen the deep affection and pride growing. Grant Ingram was a man who *should* have had a son. Though he had never, up until that moment, spoken of it Claudia had been aware of his sense of loss. A man like her father needed a son to follow after him; a son to inherit all that he had built up. Though she had always been an excellent student and majored in Fine Arts at university she had not inherited her father's gift. She loved houses and architecture and anything to do with the Arts, but she had no *special* ability. As the only daughter of a rich and cultured man she had been taught all the extras. She moved beautifully from long years of ballet, she spoke beautifully as was expected of her and doubly secured from Speech and Drama; she played the piano extremely well. She also played tennis, golf and squash. She rode well and she could swim like a fish. She did most things well but she could never take over where her father had left off. She was a girl. A precious ornament. There had never been, nor was there now, any pressure put on her to shine and succeed. It was enough that she had inherited her mother's blonde beauty and graceful manner. There was no need for her to make her own mark. Her father would leave her very comfortably off. *He* had made the money. *She* could spend it. It would have been a far different story had she been a boy. Her father would have expected great things of a son. He would, most probably, have been hard on him. Claudia was valued differently. It was her goal to marry someone like Nick so her father would have the son he had always wanted. Claudia did not begrudge her father his deepest wish. She understood his unfulfilled longing and could have wept for him. But Nick had always been out of reach. And now? Her idol had fallen.

Claudia turned away from the balustrade and walked back into her bedroom. She was seized by the most powerful melancholia, an intense desire to turn back the clock. It would be a difficult evening to get through. She could not possibly disappoint her father. He had gone to so much trouble and expense. Even Cristina, perhaps guiltily, had made a great effort to help out.

Cristina.

At first she had been rather shocked her father had married a woman nearly twenty years younger than himself. 'Mind you, love, they all do!' Fergy had said. Grant Ingram had told them he was marrying Cristina a short week before the actual ceremony. 'None of our business, I expect,' had been Fergy's next comment. 'I daresay the real reason is, he's hoping for a son.'

A *son*. How wonderful! A little brother. Immediately Claudia had felt better. But in four years, Cristina had refused point blank to stay home from her thriving interior design business and Claudia could swear her stepmother was scared silly of having a child. Once when Claudia had remarked happily that a mutual friend was expecting a baby, Cristina had exclaimed: 'How *dreadful*!' Cristina was a very glamorous creature. Not beautiful nor even strictly good looking, but impeccably elegant. For Cristina there would be no babies to perhaps ruin her tall, reed slim figure. Most people thought Cristina was a very impressive looking woman but strangely enough Nick had never looked impressed, though his penchant for mature women had always been too obvious. Beautiful women seemed to flash in and out of Nick's life, but he didn't seem to have much time for young girls.

'I really can't stand their conversation,' he had once told Claudia lightly. 'Except you, Claud, darling, and you're that way because you're your father's daughter.'

Yet in the midst of it, Nick and Cristina had had an affair.

Claudia became aware she was staring sightlessly at her reflected figure. She willed herself to pay attention. Her dress was exquisite. A rustling silk taffeta, ribboned and ruffled, the tiny bodice strapless, the skirt tiered to the floor, exaggerating the narrowness of her waist and making her look very feminine and fragile. This was the way her father liked her to look. At her ears she wore his present: diamond and pearl drop earrings. They were superb. She had intended wearing her mother's pearls around her throat but decided at the last minute they were too much. Her skin was already lightly gilded by the sun and her eyes looked very green, taking on the depth of the glossy leaves that sprayed out from the white camellias. She looked the very picture of innocence yet she was guilty of downright hatred in her heart. Hatred and deceit.

Yet how could she tell her father? 'Look here, Daddy, the Nick you love so much is sleeping with your wife.'

Claudia laughed aloud in a paroxysm of grief and irony. They'd both been super discreet since then. Nick took good care never to be left alone with Cristina for a moment. There was no use thinking about what they could manage when every back was turned. Grant Ingram suspected nothing and his daughter, burning with anguish, kept quiet. Yet the nightmare of that June afternoon came regularly . . .

Nick's car wasn't in the drive or the garage so there was nothing to warn her. She was home early from university thrilled with the 'excellent' on a rather difficult assignment that had just been handed back to her. With a few extra hours up her sleeve she intended to get in a game of tennis at the club. She ran up the stairs and used her own key on the front door so as not to disturb Fergy. Her father called Fergy their major domo. She was much more than a housekeeper. Fergy had been responsible for the smooth running of the househoold since Claudia's mother had been killed in a freak riding accident when Claudia was barely seven. Fergy had come with Miss Victoria and she had remained to look after her beloved Miss Victoria's daughter. In the Ingram household Fergy was a very special person indeed. Not even Cristina had been able to change that. Not that she tried very hard. It suited Cristina as well to have someone as dedicated and competent as Fergy to look after a very large house and garden, do the hiring, firing, answer the routine mail. Cristina had her own life and Fergy had the admirable knack of disappearing when she wasn't wanted. After he and Cristina had been married Grant Ingram had built Fergy her own self-contained bungalow in the large garden so Cristina would have no sense of sharing her home with another woman. He had talked it over with Fergy first and Fergy had told him bluntly it would suit her as well. 'I just hope, for God's sake, when I come home late one night, I remember.'

Fergy would probably have had a heart attack had she chanced on Nick and Cristina that winter's afternoon. Fergy's manner with Cristina was always crisply friendly, but she had the greatest affection for Nick. Seeing Nick with Cristina would have blown her mind. But Fergy, that afternoon, was visiting a nursery with Bill, their gardener, as Claudia belatedly remembered, which accounted for the extreme quietness of the house.

Claudia often wished afterwards she had called out. Her own relationship with Cristina was friendly enough and she had seen Cristina's smart, new Mercedes coupé in the garage (a present from her trusting husband), but up the stairs she went, her own life so crowded with activities she often acted as though she didn't have a moment to spare.

Just as she reached the first landing she saw Nick coming very quickly along the gallery and she had looked up at him in blank astonishment. He was singularly handsome. Very tall, very lean, very dark except for eyes that at times could look like pure silver. No one had Nick's quality. The authority. Yet as Claudia watched him she was surprised by the grimness of his demeanour. It even gave her a momentary pang of fear. So *that* was how Nick could look! For her, he always smiled.

They were almost on a level before he saw her and he recovered in an instant, startlingly charming while the world spun around her. For even as he spoke, Cristina came running along the gallery crying out his name. Not Nick as they all called him but, *'Dominic!'* with ardour and quickened breath. Cristina with a mist-green silk robe half falling off her, her body trembling, her hazel eyes filled with tears.

Claudia knew she would never forget it if she lived to be one hundred years. She could even recall the fragrance Cristina had worn that day and never since. It was so terrible. So shocking. So wrong. Nick and his fatal charm. Nick without dignity. Without humour.

With his figure swimming uncertainly before her eyes, Claudia had reacted, over-reacted, and Nick had told her bitingly he wasn't going to be damned by a schoolgirl's hasty judgment. She wouldn't forget that either. For all her surprisingly poised manner Claudia knew he had divined her secret; she had a very tender feeling for him and it had always touched her he was very gentle with her. But never then. Her coolness had turned to turbulence and at one stage he had slapped her so her head flew back and cleared of its faint hysteria. And then he had tried to hold her. *Hold* her! She *hated* him. More, much more, than she despised Cristina.

'Claud, Claudia, take it calmly,' he had urged her, his mouth near her ear, but she had broken away from him, white-faced while Cristina in her beautiful robe had cried over and over again Claudia was mistaken.

But Claudia had known. Perhaps she had always known since Cristina had first laid eyes on Nick. Then her startled gaze had flickered and fallen. 'I mean he's *too* much!' she had drawled to Claudia afterwards, but to the sensitive and perceptive Claudia it was easy to see she was unusually excited. Where her husband was all sweetness, Nick was certainly spice. Nick, the fallen angel.

It was the end that day of a girlish passion; the beginning of something else. The end of a carefree life; the beginning of terrible tensions. There was no anger left in her now. Only bitter disillusionment and a watchfulness that had forced her stepmother into toeing a straight line. They were all really enemies but like good actors they could assume smiles when Grant Ingram was around. What *was* life if one couldn't be civilised? What *was* infidelity for Heaven's sake!

'Claudia?' Fergy tapped on the door first, then came her head. 'Say, what's the matter, kiddo?'

'Why, *nothing*, Fergy!' Claudia turned brightly.

'You can't fool me, love.' Fergy looked at the girl very closely. 'I expect moments like these you feel a little sad?'

'Yes.'

'If only your mother had lived to see you!' Fergy circled around admiringly. 'You're not wearing her pearls?'

'I'll show you.' Claudia picked up the lustrous double strand and held them to her neck.

'Too much!' Fergy confirmed. 'I like the camellias in your hair. A lovely touch. Your daddy will be very proud.'

'I hope so.'

'Cheer up, love,' Fergy told her dryly. 'You're the precious pearl in the Ingram collection.'

'I've *other* things to offer, Fergy.'

'Hold on to that, kiddo. It's your father's nature to equate *his* women almost exclusively with looking great. If you'd been plain you would have been a terrible failure. However, you ain't. Only the servants are ugly around here.'

'*Servants!* What a stupid word. Why, this house would grind to a halt without you. We're utterly dependent on you, dearest Fergy.'

'This is *my* home, love, because it's *your* home. Anyway, your father is an important and very amiable man. Who am I to complain? Now *you*, I can understand your complaints. You're a highly intelligent girl not a beautiful doll to hang clothes on. Incidentally, the dress is ravishing.'

'You look lovely too.' It calmed Claudia just to have Fergy around and she did look most beautiful with her dear, kindly, so familiar face. She was now approaching sixty and her tanned skin was very lined but Fergy continued to radiate good humour and energy. Tonight she was wearing a most unusual creation of her own choosing, something like an Eastern robe, and her hair, usually cropped like a boy's, had been permed into a sea of little snails.

Claudia bent down and kissed her. 'I can never thank you, Fergy, for all you've done.'

'Will you *stop*!' Behind her glasses, Fergy's eyes momentarily shone with tears. 'My dearest child, you are so much like your mother, you can't imagine. I know seeing you tonight will take your grandparents back.'

'If only I'd had brothers and sisters.'

'Too late now, darling,' Fergy said. 'The next patter of feet in this house will have to be *your* children. I'm sure your stepmama will never take herself off the pill.'

Claudia had to fight not to show her sudden distaste. Cristina, she was certain, would do anything for Nick. Would she ever forget how Cristina had *looked*. The straining and the passion in her hazel eyes, nipples surging against her thin robe, the recklessness that was in her. Cristina wanted Nick with a ferocity that had made her lose her senses, betray her husband in his own house. She would do anything Nick asked of her only Nick wouldn't be asking her to leave her husband. Far from it and Claudia could even feel pity for her stepmother. Cristina might be madly in love. Nick wasn't. For Nick women were sometime alluring. His real life was tied up with plans, houses, buildings, great edifices; a whole field of endeavour far more important than making love to women. Cristina like so many before her was doomed to dismissal.

Well done, Nick!

Her grandparents were the first to arrive—Sir Ross and Lady McKinlay. Before his retirement Sir Ross had enjoyed a distinguished career as an obstetrician and had received his knighthood in the early 1970s. The same year, rather terribly, that his daughter had been killed. The blow had been enormous. Sir Ross had retired a few years after and his wife Claudia, after whom Claudia had been so joyfully named, had withdrawn from community affairs where once she had played an invigorating role. It was only in recent times that she had become reinvolved in those organisations most dear to her heart. The renewed interest and bouts of rund-raising had had a most beneficial effect on her mentally and physically. Claudia McKinlay was the kind of woman who functioned best when many demands were made upon her, but Sir Ross had been drastically altered by his daughter's sudden, early death. Where both parents had suffered, Sir Ross had been especially vulnerable. Grief had turned to a kind of despair and this had resulted in a closing off of his once wide social environment, and there was not a thing his family or his many loyal friends could do about it. Only his granddaughter could have brought him out to a large party and when he saw her coming down the stairs towards him he discovered something that miraculously eased the dammed-up desperation in his heart. He could never truly lose his daughter, she was here; Victoria's greatest achievement. Moreover she would go on through family. Claudia would marry. She had grown up so much in the last few years. Now she was a woman with a woman's miraculous body. She could have a child. His great-grandchild. For the first time in a very long while Sir Ross realised he wanted to stay alive.

'*Grandad. Nanna!*' Claudia's lovely face reflected the depth of feeling she had for these two very special people. She was so proud of them. They had done so much with their lives. Really worthwhile things. She embraced each of them in turn, looking deeply into their eyes. Her

grandmother was a tiny woman with fine bones
showing sharply through her delicate skin. She
looked ethereal until one put her to the test and
then she was streets ahead of almost anyone half
her age. Claudia always said her grandmother
would walk the legs off her. The silver-haired
fragility was all a disguise. Now she was wreathed
in smiles that nonetheless hid a few tears. Family
celebrations always had their emotional moments
and Claudia was the iving image of the daughter
they had lost. For that matter it was easy to see
where the family face had come from. Ross
McKinlay was still a strikingly handsome man
and his colouring and patrician features had been
reproduced in his daughter and granddaughter as
they would be again. It had long been one of
Claudia McKinlay's little jokes that 'all Ross's
patients fell in love with him', and for a little
while many of them had, but it was the dreamy,
idealised love that had little to do with real life.
Anyway Dr McKinlay never noticed. He was too
busy looking after his patients.

Tonight he held his granddaughter most
tenderly and the terrible sorrow that had held
him so long in its grip lifted suddenly off his
heart; an uncanny experience that he later tried
to explain to his wife, when knowing him so well
she had already divined it and thanked God from
the bottom of her heart.

By nine-thirty all the guests had arrived and
the party was in full swing. Grant Ingram had
designed his house for large scale entertaining
and the big, brilliantly lit rooms, the spacious
entrance hall and the terraces were filled with
people, laughing, talking, fooling around the

piano, dancing. Many of the guests were
Claudia's own friends, but all age groups were
represented; Grant Ingram's closest associates,
Cristina's friends, long time friends of the
Ingram and McKinlay families. All of them
mingling happily, their pleasure accentuated by
their very beautiful surroundings and the evening
dress that everyone wore.

Cristina looked particularly stunning in a one-
shouldered, toga-like garment the colour of sweet
sherry. It went wonderfully with her dark auburn
hair and her changeable, hazel eyes. Her
hollowed out cheeks and high bridged nose gave
her a look of distinction and her skin, lightly
freckled without make-up, looked flawless under
the bright lights. She was dancing with Mike
Fairholme, a T.V. personality and whatever she
was saying it had Mike's full attention. He had
even stopped dancing to be sure he caught it all.

Claudia, chilling a little, looked towards her
father's group. They were all clustered around
him almost in homage. Her father, well into his
fifties, still had a boyish look about him,
something that had to do with his wonderful
enthusiasm and working in a field of great,
cultural achievement. He had turned his head
over his shoulder to say something to Nick who
was standing with careless elegance his back
resting against the fireplace, his handsome profile
reflected in the eighteenth-century mirror. It was
almost like father to son, the expression on her
father's face, the affectionate attention Nick
accorded him. Whatever the exchange Claudia
saw her grandfather applauding and the interest
and animation in his darling, distinguished face

drove out all of the remaining chill. She had been so worried her grandfather would find this big party a trial, but somehow he seemed to be enjoying himself in a way none of the family had anticipated. Indeed she saw her grandmother reach over and clasp his hand and the smile he turned on her was sufficient to make Claudia feel a blaze of happiness. There were so many ways to love. She loved her father deeply. She adored her grandmother but a singular feeling flowed out of her to her grandfather. He looked wonderful in evening clothes. His face and tall, thin figure suited formal dress . . .

'Oh, Claudia, there you are!' A group of her friends came in from the terrace to sweep her away. So far she had only greeted Nick on arrival and there were so many people it would be possible to get right through the night without exchanging another word until he left. He was being particularly brutal to Cristina tonight, bringing Amanda Nichols with him, possibly the most decorative young widow in town, and a woman Cristina actively disliked. She would hate her now.

'Do you know you're the most beautiful creature here?' her friend Matthew Lewis told her languorously. He had danced her into a corner where there was a pocket of deep shadow. 'I think that Amanda baby is second best if you go for the older woman. They tell me old Nichols left her a packet. She must be wearing half of it around her neck. Nick's a bit of a swine bringing her, isn't he?' He went to kiss her tenderly under the ear, but Claudia drew back.

'What do you mean?'

'Oh——' Matthew looked a bit rueful now, 'one gets to be a bit bitchy on the periphery of the jet set.'

'Say what you mean.' Claudia brought up her hand and lightly hit him.

'I told you, darling, bitchiness really. Poor old Cristina is working hard to show she's not livid.'

'She has never liked Mrs Nichols,' Claudia said.

'Of course. But she's always liked *Nick*.' Matthew's blue eyes glittered as he let that drop.

'Really, Matthew . . .' Claudia felt her heart slow.

'I'm no fool, birthday girl. Come to think of it, it's quite understandable. Nick has bloody *everything*. He's spoken of at Uni as one of the *great* ones. None of us feel we can accomplish anything. Old Prof Barrett hardly ever talks of anyone else. I reckon he hangs his life on having taught Dominic Grey. And if you don't believe me . . .'

'I believe you.'

'And if that's not enough he can have any woman he wants. Lucky devil! It's a terribly elusive thing, isn't it, sex appeal? Now *you* have it. So much, I'm utterly helpless. Nick has it. God, it covers him like a shower of diamonds. Bloody unfair. Jill over there couldn't be sexy if she took off all her clothes. Yet she's a very pretty girl. You see it so many times. The haves and the have-nots. Some dangerous little chemical that's added at birth.'

'I hope you're going to restrict those kind of comments, Matt,' Claudia said, rather emotionally. 'You're talking about my father's *wife*.'

'Quite so, none of my business.' He rubbed his chin on the top of her shining hair. 'Anyway, Claudia, I'm only teasing you. I love you too much to try and hurt you.'

'You're not teasing, Matt. You're making one of your usual sharp observations. So Cristina finds Nick very attractive. She's not the only one.'

'*I'll* say! He could walk any one of them home.'

'So I don't approve of your linking their names together.'

Silence.

'Matt?' Claudia lifted her head beseechingly.

'Of course not, darling. I shouldn't have said anything. It's a good thing, mind, your father is so supremely sure of himself he's not paying much attention. Cristina's glances speak volumes. If she doesn't watch it quite a few people will become aware of how she feels. She's just walked across to Nick and put her arm through his.'

'Why shouldn't she? She's the hostess.'

'Nick looks like he's going to tell her to remove it.'

'Nick's great at putting people in their place.'

A tall, blond young man stepped in front of them. 'Say, Lewis, you can't monopolise Claudia all night. Claudia, they're playing *our* song.'

'What, from when you both went to dancing school?'

'You don't like her dancing with other fellas, do you?'

'You can read my mind,' Matthew replied.

'*Please*, this is a party.' Claudia moved away from Matthew's encircling arm and gave her hand to the determined Peter. Both young men were staring rather fixedly at each other, propelled by a faint hostility. Friends for a long time, their mutual interest in Claudia was transforming friendship into jealousy.

'I don't know why you like Matt so much,' Peter was now saying. 'I can see him being very ruthless in the years to come.'

Her father and grandfather took her in to supper. There were little speeches, of course. Many toasts. Claudia had to clear a few tears from her blazing, green eyes. While their guests were drinking coffee, her father insisted she play the piano, then settled back to enjoy his daughter's accomplishment, the romantic figure she made at the big, black concert grand, the light on her platinum hair, her slender arms and naked shoulders, the tiered skirt of her lovely dress billowing to the floor. Looking at her, he saw Victoria and he knew Claudia's grandparents would be seeing their daughter too. Something pressed on Grant Ingram's heart, some appalling weight, but he didn't allow it to settle for any time. It was all a matter of survival and he had long since perfected the knack of turning aside those intensely painful thoughts that could upset his equilibrium. Claudia was a splendid daughter and he could bask in her beauty and feminine talents. As well, she was fantastically dutiful in a day when young people challenged their parents at every turn. All in all, he was an extremely lucky man.

The champagne was flowing freely and now there were quite a few open flirtations going on.

'You played beautifully tonight, Claudia,' Cristina volunteered, gazing past Claudia's head to where Nick was leaning attentively over Amanda Nichols to hear what she was saying. Amanda was looking up at him, eyes glowing, lips parted. She wore the same, excited look Claudia had seen stamped on Cristina's face.

Another young man managed to get past Matthew's defences and whirled Claudia away. To anyone watching she appeared to be having a marvellous time. Colour flowered along her cheekbones, her eyes brilliant, her mouth was soft with laughter; her whole aura was youthful beauty. Yet inside Matthew's talk had unsettled her. There were forces loose to destroy them all. Her father was such a proud man. He had lived a life untouched by any kind of scandal. Talk of Nick and Cristina coming to his ears would deal him a terrible blow. His judgment had always been impeccable. He had chosen Cristina as his wife. He had paid Nick the greatest tribute of all. He looked on him as a son.

Her partner left her for a moment to get them both a cold drink and Claudia walked out on to the terrace, savouring the cool air. Most of the dancing couples had flocked inside. Mike Fairholme was now at the piano and Cristina, who was really very clever, was giving her impersonation of Cleo Laine. If they could *only* go back in time. Back to the time before Cristina had fallen under Nick's spell.

Claudia moved further down the terrace with Cristina's voice following her. It was a full-bodied mezzo. A *voice*, in the real sense. Why couldn't Cristina simply be happy with her father? The day they were married, she had been in floods of tears. 'Grant is the most wonderful

man in the world!' she had cried emotionally. It
made no sense at all. Indeed it was absolutely
unthinkable. And at the bottom of it, deeper even
than her fears for her father, her own bone-deep
hurt . . . the anger and bewilderment. For all his
sexual radiance she had thought Nick naturally
fastidious. There were beautiful women, certainly
but not in excess. They were more than beautiful,
they were intelligent, successful women in their
own right. No one could have called him an
addicted womaniser.

'So this is where you've run off to?' A voice
said.

She had spent most of the night hiding, now he
had found her.

'Don't you like Cristina's singing?' He joined
her, looking down at her steadily.

'I'm sort of very sensitive about Cristina,'
Claudia said.

'You mean you're a self tormentor.'

'This is *my* night, Nick,' she said.

'How you've changed.'

'Haven't we all? *Terribly*.' She turned her head
swiftly so the pearl drops moved against her
cheeks. She could feel their burning; pink flags
that would still be apparent in the muted, golden
light.

'You like to sit in judgment, Claudia, don't
you?'

'Once you could do no wrong. My father
idolises you, Nick.'

'Oh, does he really?'

'You know he does.' His voice was the most
dismal pleasure to her ears. Dark and vibrantly
cutting.

'Do you resent it?'

'No.'

'You're certainly perfect. A very beautiful girl with no faults or foibles.'

'Why don't you just *go*, Nick,' she said.

'I want to wish you a happy birthday. I haven't even given you my present.'

'I don't want any present from you and you know it.' She moved farther away from him, staring out at the garden, the shining line of the river.

'No, you prefer to press your atrocious charges.'

'You know *exactly* what I think, Nick.'

'Yes, some cruel little goddess who calmly pronounces judgment. That's really your style. Goddesses don't deal in justice or mercy. If a mortal displeases them they turn them into monsters. That's what you've attempted with me. I'm only surprised you haven't had me assassinated publicly.'

'And humiliate my *father*?' All her pent-up anger broke from her. 'Have you broken it off now, Nick, have you? Do you want forgiveness?'

'From *you*?' he caught her wrist and her heart pounded high in her throat. 'Who are you to forgive me anything. Grant Ingram's spoilt-rotten angel. What experience have you of life to judge anyone?'

'Oh, no, no, *no*, Nick. You're not going to get out of it that way. There are penalties one pays for taking another man's wife.' She knew the moment she said it she had pushed him into a terrible anger.

'What about his *daughter*?'

'She hates you.'

'I don't mind.' His handsome face was drawn into an austere mask.

'Don't you touch me, Nick,' she warned him, assailed by pure terror.

'Because you couldn't bear it, or because you really want it?'

'You're mad.' She looked behind her, seeking to escape but he closed the distance between them grasping her by the shoulders.

'No escape, Claud,' he said. 'This has been coming for a long, long time.'

'You know what I think of you.'

'I don't give a damn.' His voice was devoid of all feeling as he pulled her into his arms.

She twisted her body in a long convulsion of fear and helpless rage but it only brought her closer to lying back in his arms. '*No!*' she was screaming inside but she knew she could never use her voice. Then his mouth covered hers and the stress was too much. She went limp. Her mouth open, panting for the breath he wouldn't allow her. Sensation was spreading out through her body, shooting along her nerves. He was destroying her like the expert he was, taking her innocence in a kind of joyless triumph. She had no choice but to submit as he savagely explored her mouth, his hand hard at her back, moving her breasts against him so that she began to feel alight with a dark excitement.

'Little hypocrite,' he said harshly. 'I don't even have to coach you.' He tore his mouth away and Claudia felt so soft and faint inside she seemed to collapse against him, while he, oddly enough, gathered her closer. 'You're crying,' he said. 'You should be.'

She could feel the glitter of tears in her eyes. 'I'm crying for both of us,' she said very shakily, aware she had so little control over her body, she could not then pull away from him.

'Confusing isn't it?' he said cruelly. 'Maybe a little more experience would make you less puritanical. *Puritanical*, God,' he laughed harshly. 'Ice on the outside and a fire within. Give me women like Amanda any day. They're *exactly* what they seem.'

She couldn't understand how she could feel so frail. How unbelievable that she should be clinging to him when she was jolted through with fright and revulsion. Yet her limbs seemed to be aching for contact, one of her white arms stretched along his black sleeve, her slender body heavy against his, his arm pinning her around the waist, the other under her chin, touching her throat.

'Do you want me to kiss you again?' His silver eyes flashed. 'You're so damned good at it. Saintly little Claudia with the fabulous mouth.'

She buried her head into the curve of his shoulder. '*Don't*, Nick.'

'Oh, God, you couldn't be more *perfect*. I could kill you, Claudia. I want to after I love you. Nobody else in the whole world would treat me as you have. No one else would damn me out of hand.'

She did it without thinking at all; let her body relax against him, the need so insistent it counteracted her will. Whatever he did, however terrible, he still had this power.

'What are you doing, Claudia?' he asked tautly. 'Do you think you've found some other way?'

Lightheaded and dizzy she lifted her head. 'If I could hurt you, Nick, I would.'

'How, angel? You can't even stand by yourself.' His mouth came down, slid along her cheekbone to the corner of her lips. 'Come on, Claudia, if you want to play grown-up games.'

She gasped and went to cry out but he moved his mouth over hers, abruptly, shockingly, taking charge of her again. There was no warmth, no tenderness in this at all, but a devastating seduction performed in cold blood.

'Well, well, well, what have we here?' A familiar voice exclaimed happily.

The terrible difficulty lay in trying to speak. Claudia made an attempt and failed, being at that moment queerly disoriented. Her body couldn't even make the withdrawal from Nick's and he still held her against him with her shining skirt fanning out at the back of her.

Her father's expression said it all; a disbelieving *joy*.

'I've been trying to give her her present all night,' Nick said with a charming wryness.

'And have you?' Grant Ingram asked.

'Not as yet, sir.'

'Then I'm going to give you a chance to do so,' Grant Ingram looked from one to the other with an expression of the most intense indulgence. 'Don't be too long though, Nick. A lot of people are asking where the birthday-girl disappeared to.'

'Five minutes, Grant, and we'll be there.'

'Perfect.' He nodded to them, blue eyes glowing, and walked away.

'Oh, hell!' Claudia wailed.

'For God's sake, be *quiet!*'

'You let him think . . .'

'Okay, so what if I did?' he returned coolly. 'Your father has been living for the day when our relationship would change.'

'Oh, it's *changed*,' she said bitterly.

'Don't I know it.' He turned her so the light shone directly on her face. 'I've seen you grow from a delightful child into some terrible little avenging angel. I told you once, Claudia, that you'd made a terrible mistake but mistrust and condemnation are all I've ever had from you. Until *now*.'

She could have wept with her own helplessness. 'You wanted to bring me down, Nick.'

'Yes. You've been breathing too much rarefied air up in your ivory tower. I had thought you a frozen little witch but the heat you generate is staggering. You know what you are? You're a siren.'

'What utter nonsense! I don't belong in any such category.'

'You mean you don't *want* it to be true. You carry some idea of yourself that's shocked and outraged by the idea of passion. Your life is very cool and controlled and trouble free. You surround yourself with the sort of young men who won't endanger you. You offer them very little but that doesn't stop them falling very foolishly in love. I pity them, Claudia, because you're not at all kind.'

'And you *are*?' She looked up at him in anger and sorrow. 'I thought you cared about my father a great deal?'

'I do.' His voice was hard. 'I respect and

admire him but the fact is he's never handled you properly. If he'd treated you more as a developing human being, an emerging *woman*, instead of some perfect porcelain figurine, like the Meissen he's so fond of, perhaps you'd be somewhat different. As it is, you're rather frighteningly rigid.'

'I saw you, Nick,' she said. 'I saw Cristina. Cristina most of all. Her face openly expressed *everything*. I may have my faults, but I'm not a fool. I always felt Cristina was attracted to you, but I never, ever considered she would allow her feelings to get the better of her.'

'There was a moment tonight when *you* were abandoning all your inhibitions,' he told her brutally.

'That's different and anyway, I deny it. *I* have no husband to consider. I'm betraying no one, only myself, kissing you. I have the greatest revulsion for what you've done. Maybe you've stopped—how can I say? The fact is Nick, you and Cristina are playing with fire. If you don't care about my father, *your* career could be ruined. You may be all kinds of a genius but my father is a very influential man.'

'I have a terrible urge to strangle you,' he said quietly. 'No matter what you thought you *saw*, I am not, nor ever will be, your stepmother's lover. I do not care to go on protesting my innocence. Even for you. All this panic and anxiety you're suffering, is self inflicted. It would have to be a massive, uncontrollable passion for me to start a relationship with another man's wife. I've never met the woman who could induce that in my whole life. I've met a silly, little girl with a psychiatric disorder who could bring me remarkably close to it. But not Cristina, *no*. Cristina does *not* turn me on.'

'You want me to believe you, Nick. It's a tall order.'

'I expect tall orders from my *friends*. I know damn well you wouldn't have got such a high university entrance rating without *my* help with your maths. I spent hours with you, you little brat. You may be high on the humanities but you sure as hell have no mathematical bent.'

'No one ever explained it like you did,' she said. 'Anyway didn't I thank you over and over. Didn't I tell everyone I would never have passed without you?' Her green eyes were full of tears. 'Oh, hell, Nick,' her voice broke. 'Why couldn't you just leave well alone. There are plenty of women to love.'

'Shall I take you up on it?' he demanded harshly. 'I won't go back to Cristina if I can have *you*.'

'What, destroy me as well?' her voice rose. 'No chance of that, Nick. I want someone a whole lot better than you.' She saw the violence in his eyes and she moved back. 'But I'll offer you a deal. I'll never go to my father as long as you keep away from Cristina.'

'Did Cristina tell you about *us*?' he asked with gentle menace.

'She denied it, as you know.'

'Ah, yes. But you were determined to have a crime. Name the villain. You're not so much preoccupied with what Cristina might have done as with *me*. All in all, you're rather an interesting psychological study. Are you determined to drive me out by fair means or foul?'

'I don't know what you mean.' Her lovely face was pale.

'Oh yes you do.' His eyes held her fast. 'I don't think there was ever a time I couldn't have picked you up and put you in my pocket. You were the most breathtakingly sweet little girl. I think when I first saw you, you stopped my heart. So gentle and sweet and serene. One thick, white-gold plait and big, wonderful green eyes. You were very special then. Now you're a terrible disappointment.'

Claudia was almost afraid to speak. He looked so grim and bitter. 'We must go in, Nick,' she said. 'We're being missed.'

'As to that,' he said acidly, 'it might be helpful to stay here. I don't think your father wants anything more than to see you and me together. It would add something even more perfect to his collection.' He laughed bitterly. 'My, my, Claud, don't you look shocked. You're at pains to tell me *you're* not a fool. In all modesty *I* have a higher I.Q. We could get married. Then nine months later present your father with a grandson who would be as good as he and I put together. I know, darling. I *know*. Your father much as he loves you only has a tiny glimpse of *you*. He's one of those men who, in the most charming way possible, relegates women to the traditional, secondary role. *Service* is all very well. I don't think he really sees any point in a woman unless she is beautiful or like Cristina has the knack of presenting herself as very glamorous. There are no women associates in the firm. Jane Newcombe had to go to Harmann's.'

'Jane is a friend of yours,' Claudia defended her father's decision half-heartedly.

'Jane is a fine architect and she graduated top of her class. It was *our* loss. I told Grant this, but he brushed it aside. Positions should go on *merit*. You don't seriously think your father would have taken me on if I hadn't worn the old school tie. It helped too to have Lang Somerville as a grandfather. I'm only being realistic, Claudia. As fine an architect as your father is, he only works with people who are socially listed. He only employs people with a substantial background.'

'That *can't* be true!'

'What would *you* know? You've led a very privileged life to say the least. Jane has had to fight for everything she's got. You know nothing about battles. You've had no shaping at all. Your father might as well pick you up and shove you in one of those display cases he had built—"Now here's a very valuable piece and that over there is my daughter!" I'd choose Jane over you any day but it's not as easy as that.'

'I admire Jane, too,' she said helplessly. 'I know she's clever and tough. Do you want me to be *tough*?'

'I don't want anything from you,' he said bitterly. 'I go insane when I see you.'

'You hurt me too,' she protested, so disturbed and depressed there was an actual ache beneath her breast bone. 'Please, Nick, we must go inside. It's impossible for us to talk any more. *Impossible*.'

'Then isn't it peculiar you want me to make love to you? You can't stand it, can you?'

'No.' She had to admit it. It seemed such a transgression. She could deal with Nick more easily as her hero, not a fallen idol.

'Oh, God, what a little coward you are!' He slipped his hand into his dinner jacket and when he withdrew it he was holding a small article wrapped in crimson and gold paper. 'There just isn't any way we can get out of this. Happy Birthday, my angel. It's not what you really need but it's all I'm allowed.'

'I don't want anything, Nick!' Her breasts were rising strongly upon her narrow ribs. It was quite apparent she was agitated.

'*Take* it.' The air was electric. He held it out to her and as she took it their fingers touched.

Such a weight of desire came on her, Claudia had to drop her shining head. Desire and a sickening misery. 'Thank you,' she whispered shakily.

'Little fool.'

They had scarcely moved a few feet when Cristina bore down on them separating herself from the shadows. 'Nick, Claudia, you really will have to come inside.' Her little laugh had a jangly sound. 'What on earth are you nattering about anyway?'

'Are you sure you want to know?' Nick asked, very harshly.

'Aaah!' Cristina almost wheeled back against an arched pillar. 'You're not going to be happy, are you, Claudia, until you've torn us all apart?'

'I bleed for you, darling,' Nick said very suavely.

Claudia, literally could not bear it. Without another word, she picked her full skirt up and fled. She wasn't worldly like Nick and Cristina. She was frightened of forbidden pleasures. Could one really toss infidelity off or did people like Nick and Cristina not recognise it? She could deal with nothing, *nothing*. Even Nick's kiss had tied her in knots. She brought up her hand and rubbed her mouth. It was pulsing with heat, glowing with natural colour.

'Oh there you are, darling!'

She could hear her father's voice and in the next instant he had walked through the open doorway and grasped her arm, linking it through his own. 'Well, what did Nick give you?'

'I haven't looked yet.' It sounded like a lament.

'Uum.' Her father pulled her to him and kissed her cheek. His blue eyes looked at her with pride and approval. 'I expect you want to do that on your own?'

'Yes.'

'You've never hidden your feelings with me. You're very fond of Nick, aren't you? In fact I'd say he was about your favourite person.'

'*You're* my favourite person, Daddy,' she said. 'You're the best father in the world.'

'No question about that!' He laughed, highly pleased. 'Now where did Cristina get to?'

'She'll be here in a moment.' Claudia tried not to stiffen her body.

'I never realised she was so clever,' Grant Ingram murmured and drew his daughter back into the throng. 'Everyone really enjoyed her performance. Your grandmother was even trying to talk her into being the star turn at one of her functions. But you know Cristina. She absolutely refuses to be pinned down.'

At the sound of their approach, many heads turned.

'Grant, over here!' A woman's voice called. 'You've got to settle this argument.'

'Claudia.' Matthew was by her side. 'Mind if I sweep your daughter off, Mr Ingram?' he smiled.

'Enjoy yourselves,' Grant Ingram returned the smile benignly. Matthew was an utterly suitable young man but he wasn't for Claudia. 'Shall I take Nick's present for you, darling?' he asked. 'I'll just pop it in my pocket and give it to you after.'

Claudia's lovely face flushed pink. She passed the small package to her father and all the time Matthew didn't take his eyes off her. In a sense Grant Ingram was too self-absorbed to see the change in Claudia but Matthew did. She looked staggeringly beautiful and a little wild all at once. Something had taken possession of her. Someone. Matthew took Claudia's arm, his bright eyes darting around. A tall man came in from the terrace. Nick Grey. He too glanced across the room finding Claudia at once.

'So!' Matthew thought violently. 'If you think Claudia's going to be one of your casualties, Nick, you've got another think coming.' The muscles in his arm jumped and his expression tightened. For two years now he had been Claudia's friend. He had wanted her like crazy for all of that time. Now as he looked at Nick Grey's handsome, intense face he was shocked by his own jealousy. Claudia would need a little more convincing to see what kind of a man Dominic Grey was. There was always a great deal of talk about Nick. He was that kind of man.

CHAPTER TWO

EVEN with the Finals of her Honours course coming up, Claudia continued to go into the gallery. For the past two years she had been working *and* learning at a well-known art gallery run by Marcus Foley, connoisseur and patron of the arts, champion of the gifted unknowns and widely recognised as one of the most successful dealers in the country—certainly the most colourful. Marcus had once been a talented painter himself but once he recognised his own fatal facility he had turned his abundant energies to dealing and helping more gifted artists to achieve recognition. Therein lay his true genius and Marcus was enormously loved and revered.

Monday was the one day he allowed himself off and that was the day Claudia found herself a steady job; Monday, all day and Fridays until nine o'clock, though she never managed to get off until ten thirty or later. Not that she ever objected. What she was doing wasn't really a *job* at all. She *loved* it and she was very fond of Marcus who had been cast by nature in the baroque, rococo mould, or so it always seemed to Claudia. Yet Marcus had told her as a boy in England he had been violently unhappy though he never explained it other than to say he was always too small, too thin and too delicate to ever please his father. It had been his mother, apparently, who had sent him on a long holiday

to her sister in Melbourne. During that pleasant
stay when he managed to grow a foot and never
suffered one asthmatic attack he expressed a
desire to remain in Australia. His aunt, a maiden
lady and a very *good* artist, had been delighted
and promptly sent her sister a cable explaining
the climatic conditions were having a surprisingly
beneficial effect on Marcus.

His parents had not answered at once though
Marcus and his Aunt Estelle waited patiently, but
eventually his father wrote to say Marcus could
always come back if he wanted. He did in fact
return when his gentle little mother died or as
Marcus put it 'gave up' and his father had only
dimly recognised him then. In the intervening
years Marcus had turned from an undersized
twelve-year-old with a mop of light, fuzzy curls
into a tall, handsome, flamboyant creature who
could have stepped from a virtuoso painting
depicting a very dashing and debonair young man
of fashion.

But even then his father could not accept him
easily. 'The only thing I actually got out of him
was I had turned into something *vulgar* which
was somehow to be expected now I had attached
myself to "that idiot Estelle".' At that point,
apparently Marcus had blazed into anger, socked
his father and leapt on to the first boat home.

Thirty years later he was still wonderfully
impressive. He had legions of friends because he
was extraordinarily kind and generous and he
enjoyed people; probably women more. He had
survived two jumbled marriages and he lived in the
golden hope of finding, even now after all these
years, the perfect mate. Certainly it was possible.

There was no end of charming, flirtatious unattached women who wouldn't let him alone.

Claudia had to deal with one that very morning. Helen Villiers was a large, handsome lady who didn't really care about all the paintings she bought except it gave her the opportunity to talk to Marcus.

'Marcus not in, dear?' She went to the door of Marcus' very grand office and peered in as a double check.

'Not Mondays, Mrs Villiers,' Claudia smiled. Marcus had once been known to crawl under his massive desk to avoid detection by that very lady.

'How silly of me, I forgot.'

'Could *I* help you?' Claudia stood up and came around her own exquisite little bureau plat.

'I was just passing, you know,' Mrs Villiers lightly fanned her rose-scented body. 'I saw your stepmother the other day. I'd like to know her secret for always looking so special.'

'Effort and she's very well organised,' Claudia said.

'I fear I interrupted her—*lunch*. Nick Grey is still with your father isn't he?'

'Yes, of course.' Claudia kept her face cool and pleasant. 'Was Nick having lunch with Cristina?'

'I do hope I haven't let the cat out of the bag?' The slightly prominent blue eyes bulged.

'I'm not altogether sure what you're trying to say,' Claudia murmured, moving slightly away. She detested bitchy, troublemaking women and she had not thought Helen Villiers was like that until now. 'Cristina and Nick are quite friendly. He is always at our home. I don't see anything in the least unusual about their lunching together.'

'Of course not as she's so *happily* married.'

It was like receiving an unexpected blow in the stomach. 'You surely haven't come here, Mrs Villiers, just to tell me all this?'

'Good Lord, *no!*' Helen Villiers gave an odd little grimacing smile. 'How many women do *you* know mad about Nick Grey? Don't think I *blame* your stepmother for looking so ... so *unguarded*. He's an extraordinarily sexy man. I thank God he's much too young for me.'

'This is really a ridiculous conversation,' Claudia said. 'I don't know what Nick and my stepmother were discussing when you happened upon them but I'm pleased to tell you it could only have been something quite innocent. Probably Cristina fears my father is over-working. In fact this is very much the case at the moment. There's a very big project they're working on.'

'I've heard of it,' Helen Villiers returned blandly and Claudia saw her eyes widen as the entrance alarm sounded then someone came in the main gallery door.

'Why, hello!' Cristina stood there wearing a superb black linen suit teamed with an exquisite white blouse, very simple, very expensive gold jewellery, impeccably made-up, her mane of dark auburn hair wonderously arranged, an absolute stunner.

'Why that's quite spooky!' Helen Villiers laughed gayly. 'We were just speaking about you.'

'Really?' Cristina raised one delicately painted brow. 'Oh, do go on.'

'I was just saying how marvellous you always look!' Helen Villiers eyed the younger woman archly. 'The other day for instance, when you were having lunch with Nick Grey, I said to the people I was with, "Cristina Ingram *must* be the best dressed woman in town." I'm sure you spend a fortune on your clothes.'

'Rubbish!' Cristina said curtly. 'I spend a lot of time *planning* my wardrobe. I *don't* spend my time buying almost anything my eye falls on,' her hazel eyes swept Helen Villiers' over-dressed, matronly figure, 'and I don't indulge in a lot of torrid gossip. I believe you've told quite a few people you saw me having lunch with Nick Grey as though it was a cause for general concern?'

'Well it *was* a titillating scene,' Helen Villiers didn't falter although her firm cheeks flushed.

'Oh, *please*, Mrs Villiers,' Claudia intervened. 'This is most distasteful and really none of your business.'

'I expect you're very unhappy about it all the same.'

'Oh, look here!' Cristina said aggressively. 'We're not—I'm not and neither is Claudia— interested in your tawdry brand of gossip. I'm very fond of Nick, we *all* are.'

'You must be. You were touching him all the time.'

'I beg your pardon!' Cristina paled and for the first time her freckles became apparent.

'This is really rotten, Mrs Villiers,' Claudia said. 'Why are you interfering in our lives, acting so maliciously? Do you feel spiteful towards my stepmother and, if so, for Heaven's sake, why? I'm sure she's done you no harm. You scarcely know her.'

'I know *of* her. That is important.'

'And what does *that* mean?' Cristina almost shouted. 'You may very well regret this. I've never done anything I've been ashamed of in my life.'

'Obviously you think nothing of breaking up marriages,' Helen Villiers cried with a kind of suppressed venom. 'Do you know a Louise Baker?'

Cristina's own look of anger retreated in perplexity. 'I don't think so. *Should* I?'

'You don't know her husband Martyn?'

'Good grief, that cad!' Cristina shrugged him off contemptuously. 'What has all this to do with me?'

'Louise Baker is my niece.'

'My God, I hope she's not as boring as you are,' Cristina cut in furiously. 'It's true Martyn Baker caused me some embarrassment at one time with his highly unwanted attentions, but eventually I had him slung off my premises on his ear. I detest men who confuse pleasure with business and now that I think of it it might be as well to put you in hospital for a few weeks.'

'How *dare* you!' the older woman tottered backwards in alarm.

'I think an apology is in order, Mrs Villiers,' Claudia grasped Cristina's arm meaningfully. Cristina's hazel eyes were positively glittering and there was a high flush on her cheekbones. 'I think you were quite wrong about your niece and I *know* there is nothing reprehensible about a little show of affection. Nick Grey is as a son to my father which pretty nearly makes him *family* to us.'

'You swear you had no squalid little affair with my niece's husband?' Helen Villiers cried tersely.

'God give me patience!' Cristina returned grimly. 'Just who do you think you are, madam, the public executioner? Martyn Baker is a common weazel, not a gracious, refined person like yourself though it seems you'd hang any poor devil who so much as looked at me. In essence he or your niece is a liar. Are you grasping what I'm saying?'

'Louise told me . . .' Helen Villiers stuttered.

'Louise is an idiot. Martyn Baker might be carrying on with half the town but not me. He came to me with some story about redecorating his home and of course I took him perfectly seriously. I get such enquiries all the time. Later I realised he was just wasting my time and had him tossed out by a Swedish friend of mine. He's the bouncer from over the road,' Cristina laughed harshly. 'As to having lunch with a good friend of the family's!'

'*Please.*' All at once Mrs Villiers seemed defeated. 'My niece has been so wretched. The anguish!'

'And we do feel sorry for her and for you, Mrs Villiers,' Claudia said rather tartly, 'but you do see you've made a terrible mistake.'

'I do.' Helen Villiers shed a tear in front of them, then she turned to Claudia appealingly. 'You won't tell Marcus, will you?'

'She certainly won't. *I* will.' Cristina glared her rage across the table. 'If you expect pity from me you won't get it. By the sound of it you've been going around the town trying to destroy my reputation.'

'No, *no!*' Helen Villiers threw out an arm towards Claudia. 'Tell her that's not so. I was merely having a discreet word in *your* ear.'

'Let me see you off, Mrs Villiers,' Claudia said. 'I expect we all make foolish mistakes at times.'

'I always felt you were such a *sympathetic* girl,' Mrs Villiers allowed herself to be drawn away. 'Marcus is totally devoted to you.'

'Wicked old bitch!' Cristina cried out in a ringing tone just as they reached the bottom of the stairs.

'I really did mean it about Nick Grey and your stepmother,' Helen Villiers suddenly said. 'I might have been wrong about Martyn, I suppose, he's such a degenerate character, but I know what a woman looks like when she's in love. Friend of the family indeed!'

'I am asking you, Mrs Villiers, not to discuss this.'

'Exactly.'

'My grandmother always says if you can't say something good about someone don't say anything at all.'

'Your grandmother, if we are speaking about Lady McKinlay, is far above your stepmother.' Helen Villiers replied.

'Ugly, unfounded rumours could hurt *all* my family.'

'Well, I suppose . . .'

'Would you like me to give a message to Marcus?'

'Yes, dear.' Helen Villiers sighed and slipped behind the wheel of her car. 'I'm going away for a few days. I fear this has been all too painful. I'll ring him when I get back.'

Claudia could not bring herself to wave the woman off. Yet, however meddlesome Mrs Villiers was, she was no fool. It was getting to the stage where Cristina would have to wear a mask around Nick.

'Has the horrible old bitch gone?' Cristina demanded to know.

'Yes. I wish that hadn't happened. Mercifully no one came in to buy a picture.'

'I wanted to put one right over her head.'

'Damn it, Cristina,' Claudia cried. 'Can't you see what you're doing is dangerous? Are you going to throw up a good marriage, a good husband, so you can have some insane little affair with Nick?'

'Oh my dear . . .' Cristina blinked the furious tears back.

'I can't *believe* this of you. Of both of you,' Claudia exclaimed with appalled reproach. 'Daddy thinks the *world* of Nick. He thinks you're a very stylish lady. His *wife*. I think the shock would kill him.'

'It's my fault. All *my* fault,' Cristina said. 'God, don't you think I hate myself? Once I used to take a hard moral stand about things like this. I saw other women as being simple-minded fools but then I fell in love. I tell you, Claudia, I'm *spellbound*. I don't want to be, but I *am*.'

'You don't *love* my father?' Claudia asked in anguish.

'Of course I love him.' Cristina held a finger to her heavily mascaraed lashes. 'It's possible to love *two* men at the same time. What I feel for Grant is quite different. It's a beautiful relationship. I can see what I feel for Nick is a sin.'

'I certainly hope so,' Claudia moaned with heavy irony. 'You could wreck your whole life. I don't want to hurt you, Cristina. We were getting on quite well, but I must point out that Nick is not as committed to you as you are to him.'

'I know that.' Cristina was trying desperately not to cry. She had to go straight to work and she could not possibly ruin her makeup. 'There's no need to point it out, Claudia.'

'I think there is.' Claudia's young face was shadowed and upset. 'It must be pretty awful to fall desperately in love with the wrong person, but I suppose honour must help. You don't want to hurt Daddy, do you? Break up your marriage?'

'I wish I were dead!' Cristina said violently.

'I'd choose fighting it out any day. I feel sorry for you, Cristina, but I'm on my father's side. He would be badly stricken if some rumour came to his ears. He's not a jealous man but I think he'd be extremely *final* if he ever found out. You'd be on your own. You don't really believe Nick would go on seeing you?'

'Why couldn't he have been a perfectly *ordinary* young man?'

'My father would never have become interested in him. You must realise Daddy only surrounds himself with exceptional people. He believes you to be exceptional and it's quite true you're a very clever woman. You run your own business and you're very good at it. You look stunning and Daddy loves that. If you want your life to follow a certain style you'd better start telling yourself Nick is poison.'

'And what about you, Claudia?' Cristina asked oddly, a bitter little smile twisting her glossy mouth. 'You've been excessively attached to Nick ever since I can remember.'

'Not any more.'

'Disgusted with him, are you?'

'Yes I am. If you don't mind I'd rather not talk about Nick.'

'All right.' Cristina picked up her handbag. 'I daresay you're in love with him. Most women are.'

'Why did you come here?' Claudia asked. Cristina, although she enjoyed Marcus' company, rarely came to the gallery.

'I can't really talk to you at home. You're so *pure* and remote.'

'I also care what happens to you, Cristina,' Claudia said. 'We're not all that close but I do like you and admire you for your ability. You just can't imagine how I felt that afternoon . . .'

'You're such a child, Claudia. An adolescent. Wait until desire takes hold of you.'

'Maybe that's exactly what it is,' Claudia answered soberly. 'Desire. Not love. Love shouldn't be something frightfully destructive.'

'Well it *is*.' Cristina's whole reed slim body conveyed her titanic helplessness. 'Will you be in to dinner tonight?'

'No, I told Fergy, I'm going over to Grandad's tonight. Nanna has a meeting and I'm going to keep him company.'

'Then give him my love,' Cristina said with perfect sincerity. 'That woman has made me feel quite sick.'

'Me too.'

'Make yourself a cup of tea.' Cristina wiggled her fingers over her shoulder. 'I hope Marcus is going to join us Saturday night. He's such marvellous company.'

Claudia stared after her stepmother with an

expression of almost theatrical perplexity. 'I'll leave him a reminder.'

'Good, dear. Take care. Remember what Marcus always says. If some lunatic comes in with a sawn-off shotgun and demands some of the paintings, let him have the lot.'

'I'll remember,' Claudia muttered in a strangled voice. These days she wasn't all that sure what *lunatic* meant. If she *had* to pick a word that best described her stepmother's behaviour it would have to be schizophrenic. Cristina was only in her early thirties so it couldn't be some raging hormonal imbalance, a mad desire to stave off loss of desirability with a particularly white-hot affair. This was actually Cristina's *second* marriage. Her first had ended abruptly at the age of twenty-four, the reason being, according to Cristina, her husband had been 'a terribly dull guy'. First of all, he was an accountant . . .

It was a slow day altogether after a very profitable weekend but towards late afternoon Marcus called in and everything blossomed for an hour.

'You seemed a little depressed when I came in,' Marcus observed in his wonderfully fruity voice actually handed on to him by his father.

'I suppose I was.' Claudia ran her fingers with absent reverence over a MacKennal bronze that had recently cropped up in a convent where it had served as a kind of paperweight. Reverend Mother had thought it a bust of the Madonna but when told that it was not had no objection to selling it to Marcus for an undisclosed price.

'Anything I can do?' Marcus looked up at her

from beneath his Mephisthophelean eyebrows. 'I'm fond of solving knotty problems.'

'Very good at it too,' Claudia smiled. 'No, I don't think so, Marcus dear.'

'In love, are you?'

'Why ever would you say that?' Claudia burst out after a moment of profound silence.

'Come, come, Claudia,' Marcus looked at her with an expression of sympathy and a smile. 'I was at the party remember?'

'So?' She knew she was flushing badly.

'My dear child, I've known you since you were a little girl and your father used to bring you in with him so you could develop an "eye" early. I know every expression on your face. I know when you're happy, sad, worried and depressed. I also know when someone in particular is causing you a little heartache. Someone who has been at the centre of your life for a long time now. Someone *I* see as absolutely ideal for you.'

'You're wrong, Marcus,' Claudia shook her head.

'As a matter of fact, I'm not.' Marcus glanced quickly through a letter, then tore it up. 'Should have really stamped on it,' he muttered distastefully then returned his glance to Claudia. 'Nick cares about you a great deal.'

'Who says so?'

'My dear, I *know*. I should think everyone knows. Your father thinks the world of him, that's so, isn't it?'

'He would have liked Nick as a son.'

'Well, I wouldn't be unhappy with a son like that either,' Marcus said mildly. 'The question is, dear girl, is it making you a little bit jealous?'

'Marcus!' Claudia's emerald eyes opened wide. 'You must be mad!'

'All right then,' Marcus spread his large, shapely hands. 'We have a mystery here. What is the problem?'

Claudia turned her head away. Nice as Marcus was, she couldn't tell him. 'I think Nick sees me as a little girl,' she side-tracked. 'He's quite a bit older and he has *never* been interested in my age group. Young girls have terrible conversation.'

'Quite right, they do, but they're so *pretty*!'

Claudia shook her head again, shoulders drooping, eyelashes coming down on her cheeks.

'Listen, my little one, your conversation is really very good. Incidentally *I* must take a little credit for it.'

'Of course.'

'Don't be cheeky.' Marcus turned away to check the security system. 'I'm not sure what's gone wrong between you and Nick but I wouldn't allow it to keep up if I were you. I think possibly Nick has *had* to get used to thinking of you as a child, or a young relative or whatever. It would never have done, for instance, not to allow you to grow up, finish off your education, allow yourself plenty of young admirers.'

'Marcus, *stop*. Turn around here and tell me what you're talking about?' Claudia pleaded.

Marcus did turn around, shaking his leonine head. 'I believe, my dear, you've got to work it out for yourself. Perhaps that would be best.' He reached out and touched Claudia's shoulder. 'What did dear old Shakespeare say? "We that are true lovers run into strange capers".'

'*As You Like It*,' Claudia confirmed sighing. 'Speaking of strange capers, Mrs Villiers was in this morning.'

'Dear Lord!' Marcus' large, pleasantly rounded form shook from head to foot. 'Surely she knows I'm not in Mondays?'

'Probably forgot.'

'You didn't say where I was?' Marcus walked about, turning off the lights.

'So she could go out searching? No.' Claudia moved to help him. 'Actually she just wanted you to know she's going away for a few days.'

'That's scarcely *my* business,' Marcus said mildly. 'Why can't women be happy on their own?'

'How can *anyone* be happy on their *own*, Marcus? We must have someone to love. You have wonderful friends.'

'For which I'm intensely grateful.' Marcus stroked his luxuriant moustache. 'I can't say I blame her for chasing me. I'm an awfully good catch.'

This had the effect of making Claudia laugh wildly and after a moment Marcus joined her. 'Seriously, Claudia, I *am*,' he gasped when they sobered. 'Now, as you're going out to your grandfather's I'll put the De Maistre in the boot. It's a very interesting work. We were lucky to get it. It was sold at Christie's at the end of '74. Burnett wouldn't let it go until now.'

Marcus locked up and they walked in a companionable silence out to Claudia's little run-about. 'Have you arranged about the flowers for Friday?' Marcus asked, as he settled the heavy painting into the boot. Friday evening they were having a showing of Allan Brunton's new works; brilliant canvases alive with the birds and flowers of tropical North Queensland.

'Actually I didn't ring the florist this time. I rang the nursery. All the cymbidiums are out and I thought they'd look marvellous in baskets about the place. They'll pick up the theme of the paintings as well.'

'Good girl! So beautiful and so capable. Do you know neither of my wives cared about having children and one simply can't be happy without children.' For a moment Marcus' heavy, handsome face was lost in melancholy, then it faded into something else. 'You didn't forget the Dixons, did you?' He held open the car door and Claudia slid in.

'I haven't forgotten a thing. At least I hope not. Remember Dr Kempf will be coming in in the morning.'

'Will she the old vixen!'

'She's a highly regarded critic.'

'Give me a man any day. They're easier to deal with.'

'You love women, Marcus.' Claudia turned a smiling face to him. ''Bye, now. See you Friday. I've left all my little notes for Jean. The orchids will arrive Friday morning. They're going to set you back a bit, but they'll look magnificent and we can always use them again.'

Marcus leaned over and kissed her on the forehead. 'Say hello to your grandfather for me. I was so pleased to see how much he enjoyed the party.'

'Yes he did, didn't he?' Claudia could still see her grandfather's eyes on her as she had come down the stairway. 'I really think his great sadness is passing.'

'Maybe he's seeing great promise for the future,' Marcus said perceptively. 'And that promise is in *your* hands. Which brings me back to Nick. Don't let misunderstandings get in your way. Nick no longer sees you as a small girl. Take my word for it. Why shouldn't you be his *wife*?'

'For one thing, he doesn't love me,' Claudia suddenly started the engine. 'And another, Marcus, you old matchmaker, I certainly don't love him.'

'It might help you to put it in gear.'

'Yes.' Claudia shifted the gear stick into Drive. 'I do hope Nick won't come on Friday.'

'Of course he'll come!' Marcus waved her off, having the last word. 'Nick wouldn't miss one of my showings for the world.'

CHAPTER THREE

A CROWD was fast gathering and Claudia motioned to one of the hired waiters to circle with drinks. That done, she paused, her eyes scanning the large gallery. The cymbidiums looked superb; pink, white, yellow, a very pale green and a rich, rust-red. The abundant flower spikes on some were easily five feet long and she could see from Marcus' beaming face they were proving just the decoration for the Brunton showing.

Above the exotic, waxy opulence of the flowers, the paintings radiated the splendours of the tropical North. As with Gauguin, colour was the *raison d'être* of Brunton's work and he had devoted the last four years of his working life exclusively to catching the atmosphere north of Capricorn; the peculiar brilliance of the light, the sheer abundance of flora, the flaring colours, the myriads of birds like precious jewels. Several of the largest paintings were already displaying reassuring red stickers; not that Allan Brunton, a man as spectacular as his paintings, needed all that much reassuring. Claudia had already overheard his declaiming to a lad who sought to enage him in conversation that he 'didn't give a damn whether anyone bought his paintings or not'. With another artist one might have wept torrents but such was Brunton's rank, dealer and buyer just had to laugh it off. 'Always feel he's never quite got the hang of civilisation!' Marcus often said.

One of their best clients, an enormously wealthy elderly gentleman, 'a bit on the gay side' as Marcus put it, was now whispering in his ear and several minutes later Claudia was asked to affix a 'heavenly crimson dot' to the very sumptuous No 28—'Hymn to Tropical Beauty and Fruitfulness'. The price tag was as arresting as the brilliant images and having been in the client's home, Claudia couldn't conceive of where such a very large painting might go. There was no more wall space. It was even rumoured there was some sort of gallery in the upstairs what-not. There were handsome paintings in the kitchen, scattered along the garage walls, many a guest had been known to come back enraptured from a visit to the toilet. All at once Claudia decided it wasn't her job to worry where the client's pictures might go.

Shortly afterwards her father and Cristina arrived and perhaps twenty minutes before the 8 p.m. closing time Nick called in. *Alone*. Cristina was in the middle of a sentence as Nick pushed through the crowd but as soon as her eyes fell on him, she suddenly flushed and faltered badly. That she was flustered was so obvious Claudia felt extremely uncomfortable, but the effect wasn't as bad as she feared because her father swung around rather bewildered, then exclaimed aloud in pleasure. 'Why, it's Nick! Damned if I knew what was bothering you, darling.'

'Why, of course it's Nick,' Cristina said helplessly. 'I thought a woman over there was going to tip champagne all over his sleeve, it's such a crush!'

To Claudia's way of thinking it came out too contrived for words, but apparently her father needed little convincing.

'You'll have to excuse me,' she said and gave Nick a fleeting, wintry smile.

'I think this little show is going to be a success,' he said mildly as he greeted them. 'Won't you show me around, Claudia, instead of rushing away?'

'Yes, darling, that's your job,' her father pointed out with a sharp, amused smile. 'You don't have to *buy* one, Nick. That's carrying things a bit far.'

'A bit colourful for me,' Nick murmured detachedly. 'Excellent of their kind though, one has to admit.' He half turned to look at Claudia but she kept her green eyes on the painting right in front of her. There was a snake she suddenly realised in one of those rioting trees ... brilliant eyes in a menacing triangular head.

'Where are you going afterwards, Nick?' Grant Ingram suddenly asked.

'As a matter of fact, home.' His silvery glance moved off Claudia and stopped at her father.

'Let's have dinner. Just the four of us,' Grant Ingram said. 'Cristina and I were going on but I'm sure they can find us a table for four.'

'I'll probably have to stay, Daddy,' Claudia said.

'Nonsense!' Grant Ingram's blue eyes were serene. 'Marcus won't mind in the least.'

'I don't know.'

'*I'd* like it,' Nick said and caught Claudia's hand firmly. 'Quickly, show me around before we go.'

She looked back over her shoulder as they moved off. Her father was smiling, but it was very hard to define the expression on Cristina's face.

'What can you tell me about this one?' Nick suddenly asked dryly and turned his attention to a strange, jungle scene.

'I don't *want* to go to dinner tonight, Nick.'

'Would you please speak a little louder, Miss Ingram. I can't hear you in all this din.' There was an expression of malice on his handsome, dark face.

'Don't you *care* that Daddy might notice something?'

'Why do you have to keep calling your father "Daddy" in that little-girl fashion?'

'Because that's how I think of him if you want to know.'

'Why do you have to be some sort of god-damn little paragon?' he enquired. 'A veritable child of light!'

'Like it?' Marcus came over to clap him on the shoulder.

'It vaguely upsets me,' Nick said.

'Complex chap!' Marcus said rather sadly.

'Who, me or Brunton?'

'I meant Brunton but I suppose one would have to watch *you* carefully.'

Claudia stared up at Marcus aghast but to her relief he was smiling at Nick most affectionately.

'I haven't spoken to the Randalls since they came in,' she pronounced quickly. 'Excuse me, won't you, Nick?'

'Of course. Marcus can show me around.'

'Step this way, laddie,' Marcus boomed.

Of course there was no way of getting out of dinner. Her father expected it and what her father expected, her father got. Even if it turned out to be the very last thing in the world. Like Cristina and Nick.

There was not the slightest difficulty finding the best table even on a busy night. Her father commanded attention wherever he went. Accepted it as his due. Now as they all sat at a table together his eyes wandered with pleasure from his daughter in a lovely pale jade crêpe de Chine sheath dress, hand-sewn with beads and silver sequins, to Nick, lean and elegant in his impeccably cut dark grey suit, shirt and tie expertly chosen and in the traditional, classic style Grant Ingram most admired. Nick was a handsome man. But for all that, the chiselled features, the thick, black hair and stunning light eyes, were merely a bonus. It was the brilliance of his personality, his particular abilities that made him so sought after. He had a peculiar *drawing* power. For men and for women. Even Cristina who had said Nick was 'so dazzling he was blinding' had overcome her initial reaction. She was as fond of him as the rest of them. Perhaps not *Claudia*. Grant Ingram smiled indulgently on them both. His most longed-for wish appeared to be working out very nicely.

Claudia barely tasted a morsel of food but the others ate and drank with pleasure. Cristina was particularly scintillating, as if she had an excess of nervous energy she had to burn off. Her hazel eyes even had a hint of triumph in them as they rested on her stepdaughter's still, downbent face. Claudia might be all those years *younger* but

Cristina was still the more vibrant of the two; the more interesting, the more witty, the more able to hold and keep a sophisticated man's attention. That night all her old pennants were flying. She couldn't bear to lose her husband any more than she could bear to have Nick turn away from her in boredom. Nick was the most dangerous person in the world to her. In his company she felt as much on a high as any pathetic victim of an addiction. What he represented she didn't know but it was something she had missed.

The maitre d' came over to make certain they had enjoyed their meal and afterwards Cristina suggested they might make use of the small dance floor. Several couples were moving about in languorous abandon enjoying the immensely pleasing sounds that were emanating from the four-piece group.

'You're very quiet tonight, darling?' Grant Ingram said when he and Claudia were alone.

'I'm a little tired.' She smiled at him, trying not to see Cristina and Nick over her father's shoulder. Anxiety was there again, right around her heart. Cristina was in such a brittle mood tonight the whole thing could blow up in their faces.

'You're studying too hard,' her father told her.

'No wonder, it's close to exams.'

'I'm very proud of you, Claudia,' Grant Ingram smiled. 'What are you going to do with yourself when it's all over?'

'I have a few things lined up,' she said readily enough. 'I might even travel for a year.'

'You're joking, darling,' her father said lightly. 'I can see which way the wind is blowing.'

Can you? she thought sadly. In many ways her father only saw what he wanted to.

'My advice is, darling, don't go rushing off overseas. I guess I understand how you feel about Nick. You've always been a child to his young adult, but these days it seems to me he's treating you as a *woman*.'

'That's the problem with Nick. He treats women like women and they *love* it!'

'He's never married any one of them,' her father said.

'Maybe he hates the idea of marriage,' Claudia said moodily. 'He told me once it was agony when his parents' marriage broke up. It was so bad for a time he had to go and live with his grandfather.'

Grant Ingram nodded. 'That's right. But it was a very long time ago, sweetheart. Nick was only a boy.'

'What *worse* time,' Claudia said. 'I don't think underneath all his surface charm Nick really *likes* women. He mightn't think they would be too faithful. He told me he blamed his mother for the break-up of his parents' marriage.'

'She was an extremely beautiful woman,' Grant Ingram said. 'It could be very difficult for any man to hold a woman like that. Grey is a good fellow but ultra-conservative, rather rigid in his thinking. If anything I would have to sympathise with Nick's mother. However much he blamed her he's very much like her. But that's just between you and me. Nick is all the Somerville side of the family.'

'And he's never forgiven his mother's defection.'

'What is it you're getting at, darling?' Grant Ingram asked just a shade testily. 'I think you're throwing up all kinds of silly defences. I'm totally convinced Nick is just about ready to settle down and nothing in this whole world would please me more than if he decided to settle down with *you*.'

'Why, *exactly*?' Claudia asked. 'Do you think he's the right person to make *me* happy, or is it because you love him dearly?'

Grant Ingram laughed a little ruefully. 'Every woman needs a man to take care of her. In terms of character, ability, ambition, I can't think of anyone I would rather see you married to. Do you resent my affection for Nick? Is that it, darling?'

'Ah, no,' Claudia shook her head. 'I understand the special relationship that exists between men. Father to son. Most men, I suppose, would wish for a son before a daughter. Of course they love their daughters, as you love me, but the really important thing in a lot of men's lives is to have a son. Preferably sons. It's perfectly understandable. A man relives his hopes, his dreams through a son. A lot of the time it could be a second chance. I suppose mothers do it too through their daughters but the male of the species is predestined to do great things,' Claudia shrugged a little ironically. 'I believe you think *Nick's* child, providing I was accorded the great honour of being its mother, would be the greatest architect the world has ever seen.'

'Damn it all, darling,' her father laughed. 'He *might* be. There's really a great deal to be said for mating the right couples.'

'I hardly dare mention *love*.'

'You love him,' Grant Ingram said soberly. 'I know you're still slightly in awe of him, but you're demonstrating your own style. You're a beautiful young woman. You're well educated, well bred. What more could a man want?'

'Plenty,' Claudia said fiercely, marvelling at herself for saying it. 'Actually it's *sexy* women men go for. Another woman might have plenty to offer but if she hasn't got *that* she's a non-event.'

'Personally I detest crude women,' Grant Ingram said. 'Certainly I would never marry one.'

At which point Cristina and Nick returned to the table, Cristina, flushed and brilliant-eyed, Nick looking rather taut and silent by comparison.

'I think we'll leave you two young people,' Grant Ingram said.

'But it's *early*, darling,' Cristina protested, rather tartly. She was as *young* as anyone, actually.

'I'm ready to go home,' Claudia said.

'You're not a bit of fun, are you?' Nick challenged her with a mocking smile.

'That's a little bit of her trouble,' Grant Ingram murmured and gestured to the maitre d' for the bill. 'She's too serious. No, stay here, darling and enjoy yourself. Nick will bring you home.'

'I'm enjoying myself too, you know,' Cristina told her husband, opening wide her changeable eyes.

'Don't fret,' Grant Ingram told her. 'The evening's not over. It's just that I think these two have much to say to each other.'

'Oh, God, Grant!' Cristina groaned. How could *anyone* be so blatant in their matchmaking? Claudia and Nick had nothing to say to each other. Claudia was just a baby.

Yet Nick, the traitor, reached out and grasped Claudia's hand. 'I'm hoping to persuade Claudia to dance with me.'

'She looks tired,' Cristina snapped, a tone of voice that made Grant Ingram lift his head from his credit card to frown at her.

'It's *relaxation* she needs,' he pointed out sternly.

Cristina wasn't brave enough to start up again. Grant was the most courteous and considerate husband in the world but he could be surprisingly stuffy when crossed.

'Have a lovely time!' Cristina said as they left, but her over-bright eyes made it plain she thought that impossible.

'Some days,' Claudia said, 'I feel like an old, old woman.'

'*How* old?' Nick lifted her hand to his mouth.

'Don't play games with me,' she said with icy disapproval.

'This is no place to kiss you in earnest.' His silver eyes sparkled in his handsome, dark face. 'Dance with me, Claudia? It will all be quite friendly.'

'I'm very glad my father had his back to you when you were dancing with Cristina.'

'It's a sticky problem, I'll admit.'

'You're tired of her, aren't you?' Claudia accused him, feeling so angry her hands were shaking.

'Keep that up and you might have to go in a

strait-jacket,' Nick returned rather curtly. 'Do you want to dance or don't you?'

'No. I don't want you to touch me.'

'What a wicked lie!'

'You don't seem to realise I *mean* it.'

'Hush, you little fool.' He held her hand so tightly she couldn't pull away. 'If you don't want to dance, we'd better go.'

'It's the only way.' She was already standing, one hand still in his, the other reaching for her evening purse.

There was no one in the car park. 'Get in,' Nick said briefly and with a crushing disdain.

'I should never have come.'

'I don't see what else a dutiful daughter could do,' he taunted her. 'And it's much too early to take you home. Your father is expecting us to dance the rest of the night away. One wonders why.'

Claudia wasn't listening. She was buckling her seat belt. This was the first time she had been inside Nick's new car, the Jaguar coupé and she thoroughly approved of the high console down the middle. Not that Nick had any ideas of crossing over anyway. In the lamplight his expression was one of positive dislike.

'What about my place?' he asked as the big engine fired.

'I don't *believe* you.'

'I'm serious. I'll read you a bedtime story before I take you home.'

'I'd prefer it if you skipped the story.'

'Don't be such a kill-joy. Really, Claudia, you're turning into a terribly dull girl.'

'Because I wouldn't consider sleeping with you? Sorry about that.'

'Have I *asked* you?' he drawled.

'I'm sure you would given the chance.'

'*No*. It would be sacrilege. I see you as an object of *adoration*, Claudia. You're much too fine a person to ask into bed.'

'You mean you hate wasting time.'

'You disgusting little bitch.'

Never in all the years that she had known him had he called her such a name. She wasn't a bitch. She *wasn't*. She was carrying a terribly worrying burden.

'What's the matter with you now?' he asked harshly.

She couldn't answer because she was choking on a few involuntary tears.

'I'm sorry,' he said. 'I didn't mean it. I just made it up. You're an angel with a very pure *little* mind. My place, is it? No seduction scene. No kisses, caresses, no vicious words. I'll show you the plans for the MacAdam residence. You used to be interested in things like that.'

'I want to go home, Nick,' she near-whispered.

'My poor dear child it would be much better for *all* of us if I kept you out for at least another hour. Consider your father's feelings. Cristina's. She seemed ready to explode.'

'You only *thought* she could play the game.'

'Who needs friends, Claudia, when I have you. I'm the victim of a bit of damning circumstantial evidence yet you've come down on me like a fury. Could it contain the element of a woman scorned?'

'No,' she said, sounding very young and shaken. 'I worshipped you for years and years. Another case of a fallen idol, I'm afraid.'

'For God's sake!' he said angrily and with a look of near despair, 'what the hell can I do if some fool woman finds me cataclysmically attractive? I'm as angry with the whole thing as you are. I've tried to reason with Cristina, but she persists. Maybe it's the bloody menopause!'

'What an extraordinary diagnosis,' Claudia offered flatly, 'but try saying that to Cristina for a whole month. When it actually happens and it's a good way off, she'll think there's nothing left for her. When desirability fails, go jump off a mountain.'

'A bridge anyway. If she doesn't, I'll *have* to!' He was heading towards his own home and Claudia reminded herself cynically that it would be better if Cristina and her father thought she and Nick were enjoying a long evening.

'Expecting someone, Nick?' she asked as they drove through the tall, iron lace gates.

'I always leave the lights on when I'm not at home. A simple precaution.'

'What an extraordinarily beautiful old house this is,' she said quietly. 'I always expect to see your grandfather come out to greet us.'

'Yes,' he agreed a little curtly. 'It would trouble him a great deal to know what goes on in *your* mind.'

In silence they walked to the front door, a soft golden light streaming through the patterned leadlights. It was a traditional Tudor manor house built by Nick's great-grandfather and its most outstanding feature apart from the wide swaths of leaded glass windows with inserts of European stained glass was the magnificent panelling brought intact from England in the formal dining room. The estate had passed to Nick after the death of his maternal grandfather, Lang Somerville, but it was much, much too big for one man, though Nick's grandfather had lived the last ten years of his life alone in it and quite happily. It had been his home and now it was Nick's.

'Well don't just stand there!' Nick knit his black brows.

'Oh, Nick . . .' Her voice sounded fearful and gentle.

'*I'd* never hurt you Claudia.' There was the faintest smile in his eyes. He took her hand and led her into the drawing room turning on the light at the same time. 'Do you want to stay here or go into the library. It's a darn sight cosier.'

'Aren't you going to show me the MacAdam house plans?' She looked up at him worriedly, her eyes very large and lit with a desperately controlled excitement.

'Now?'

'Yes now.'

He looked down at her trembling hand in his. 'You used *not* to be afraid of me.'

'I only wish we *could* go back to before.'

'You've no right to behave like this, Claudia,' he said.

'And how can you be so *dreadful*!' She broke away from him then. 'I can't stay here, Nick. I can't be with you at all.' An emotional tear rolled down her creamy cheek.

'Claudia,' he said bleakly, 'it's not even midnight. I'll take you home then. Can't you talk to me for an hour?'

She put put her hands to her temples, slanting her eyes back. 'I can't think of a single thing.'

He wasted no further time, closing the gap between them and wrenching her into his arms. 'Do you want me to strangle you, do you?'

'This violence is new,' she goaded him, shaken, shocked, acutely aware of the peculiar tensions that bound them.

He exclaimed under his breath. 'Is there anything else I *can* do with you?'

'Yes. Take me home.' A long pin had fallen out of her hair and now it slid in a heavy platinum coil down her back. The sight of him, the touch of his hurting hands was rousing a dark clamour in her blood, quickening into raw sensitivity her irreconcilable feeling for him.

'It makes no difference that I'm telling you you're quite *wrong*?'

'I *want* to believe you, Nick. You must know that.'

'Then there's only one way to show you.' The initiative was his and he grasped the long coil of her hair and forced her head back against his shoulder, pressing his mouth down on hers until she parted her lips on a moan of pain.

'Forget *everything* but this,' he said tautly, twisting her slender body even nearer so the pulses began beating ever more thunderously in her veins. She had imagined being kissed by Nick so often, but the reality was beyond anything she could handle. Even while her mind seethed in self-disgust, her body trembled and yielded independently, slow fire wrapping her around. He was so blindingly skilful in his heart-stopping role. A real-life sorcerer. She allowed him to explore her mouth a while longer, then with a convulsive movement she jerked her head away.

'I've got to hand it to you, Nick, you know how to make love.'

He just looked at her, hostility surfacing in his diamond-bright eyes. 'Curiously enough so do you, when I know you're still a virgin.'

'You're quite certain about that?' she snapped, points of colour staining her cheekbones.

'Yes. A virgin. Much too long.'

There was such an odd, menacing tone in his voice she closed her eyes and abruptly he lifted her, carrying her back to the wide sofa where he held her across his knees.

Tears of rage and panic dropped on to his hand. 'You promised me . . .'

'*Shut up.*' He answered so fiercely it checked her. 'You've got to understand something, Claudia. You can't goad a man beyond his limits.'

She felt his hand on her shaping her breast but before she had time to breathe or even cry out his mouth had descended again and it was far too sweet to avoid. Urgency poured into her veins so her heart thudded within her narrow rib-cage. She lifted her arms, drugged with yearning, linking them around his head so his strong body trembled with the force of his reaction.

It was like trying to tame a prowling panther and in her excitement was a measure of terror. She had known Nick for so long but he was someone else now. A lover, sexual and angry. She thought she heard her fragile dress begin to tear, but then the zip was darting down her back and with a swift motion of his hand he had peeled it from her, flinging it so it flew through the air in a shimmering haze.

'Oh, *no*, Nick!' she cried breathlessly, her

whole body suffused with heat. Without her dress in a flimsy slip she felt utterly bereft, raising one hand protectively across her body. She had always been shy with Nick. Couldn't he understand?

'I won't hurt you. Just a little,' he muttered, his lean fingers curving around her throat.

'*Nick*.' He seemed utterly unstoppable, a hard tension in his face.

'All the misery you cause,' he said grimly.

She knew in that instant he was about to seek her breast and she jerked back convulsively in a frenzy of emotion. She had never known such intimacy in her life, the terrible, awesome power of desire. She didn't think she could bear Nick's hand on her naked flesh but now her breasts were exposed and he was putting his mouth to their rosy peaks bringing her mortally, perilously within his power.

'You're so beautiful!' he murmured spreading his hands over the curve of her hips. 'All I've got to do is keep loving you.' His voice was filled with a kind of exultancy, a suppressed triumph and it burnt into her like a flame. She turned her head from side to side to clear it, shuddering as Nick brushed his hand down her body. Part of her wanted his overwhelming male aggression, the rest of her couldn't bring herself to surrender. She knew who she was. She knew what she wanted. Love and respect. Not a demonic desire.

With a tremendous effort she brought her body upright drawing her slender legs up so she was sitting like a child in his lap. 'Please stop now, Nick,' she begged him, breathing very deeply in an effort to slow her racing heart beat.

'You sound like a little girl.'

'You know I am. At least I'm——'

'Frightened?' Incredibly he was holding her in an attitude of protectiveness.

'I want the man I love to love only me.' She pressed her mouth against his throat, mournful and ardent. So stupid!

'Perhaps he does. Perhaps he's loved you for years.' He brought his hands upwards beneath her breasts, the tips of his fingers stroking the nipples.

'*Please* help me, Nick,' she whispered. When he did that her mind began to whirl out of control.

'Then tell me you believe me.' He pulled her head back so he could look into her eyes. '*Tell* me.' His silver eyes were blazing.

'I'll *try*, Nick.' Desperately she tried to appease him.

'You don't know *anything*, do you?' he asked harshly. 'No matter what you know of me you can't give me your trust. It's some deep-seated defence. Something a vulnerable little girl thought up to guard against her own longing. You've been in love with me since you were about thirteen years old.'

'*Nnn . . . no!*' She tried to pull back as he held her close to him, feeling like the victim of a mad obsession.

'You've wanted this at any time for years now.'

'No, Nick, I won't *let* you.' Her body jerked away from his hard domination.

'Sweet God!' he breathed. 'This is all more bizarre than I thought.'

With an expertise she hated he turned her and got her back into her flimsy garments, bringing her rather roughly to her feet where she stood with enormous eyes while he dropped her lovely dress over her head. He even ordered her curtly to lift her arms and turn around so he could adjust the zip. It was exactly as if she were a child or some colourless puppet.

'Now, goddammit,' he fairly shook her, 'I'm going to take you home. Is your blasted dress all right?'

'I don't know.' She looked at him so strangely, brushing tears from her eyes.

'I could beat you, Claud,' his voice sank to a whisper. 'Don't look like that, *please*.'

'I'm a disgrace, aren't I?'

'You idiot.' He brushed her heavy hair away from her face. 'You always knew I'd make love to you.'

'I think it was as hard for you as for me.'

'*Harder*, baby.' His dark face mocked her. 'You don't even know the half of it. What are you going to do about your hair?'

'Is it untidy?' She sounded frightened.

'As if it matters.' He stood there watching her very closely. 'I guess you're old enough to let your hair down.'

'I'd better fix it.' Colour emphasised the creaminess of her complexion. 'Daddy or Cristina might still be up.'

'You look fine. Leave it,' he said a little curtly. 'Seeing you kissed senseless might be good for them both.'

No one was up, however. Claudia slipped into the quiet house, turned off the exterior lights and climbed the stairs to her bedroom. Her father and

Cristina had their suite in the other wing and all that mattered now was to reach the solace of her own room. In a sense she had always known what had happened tonight. What *would* happen if she allowed Nick to carry her off to where they would be quite alone. The scent of him still clung to her; to her mouth, to her skin, to her clothes. Hers was the worst kind of obsession, instilled too early. She could still feel his hands on her breasts, demanding, strong, clever hands. She had always liked just to look at them, the beautiful shape, the expressive elegance. How incredible they had touched her body. And with such authority! How incredible she had given in at all.

Silence along the long gallery. She opened the door of her own room, flicked the light switch then turned back to find the master switch that controlled the recessed lighting in the gallery. Another second and the main house was in darkness but Claudia thought she caught the glimmer of light from the far end of the long passageway. She didn't wait to make sure but hurried back into her room.

She found the slightest tear in her dress but it could be easily mended. In the bathroooom she stopped for a moment before she slid her nightgown over her head. Normally she undressed without ever looking at herself now she turned and looked at herself in the mirror, seeing her body as a lover might. Her skin was flawless over her entire body and she relived again how hungrily Nick had reached for her, his mouth and his hands. She pressed her arms around her own body, her green eyes huge and troubled. Nothing made sense, *nothing*! Could he possibly reach for another woman with the same fervour? Could he possibly be telling the truth after she had berated him so terribly? Yet even tonight Cristina had flaunted her power, leaning heavily against him as they danced, finally disentangling her hands, her hazel eyes over-bright.

Claudia's soft mouth twisted in an expression of pain and disbelief. Was this some thoughtless cruelty of fate that Cristina had conceived a passion for a man who had merely been charming to her since she was the wife of his senior partner? It had happened before. Men and women had been known to fall madly in love without encouragement, just as they were tempted to want what they could not have.

Claudia dropped her pink nightgown over her head, reaching behind the door for her pink satin robe. Her hair was hanging long and heavy over her shoulders and she saw she looked different, pulsing with an inner light. These kinds of triangles were only for fiction. They were too terrible for real life.

A tap on her door, then the soft thud of footsteps in her bedroom made her heart leap to her throat. She hurried to the bathroom door and looked out in apprehension. Cristina in a marvellous burgundy nightgown and matching peignoir was standing in the middle of the room looking very severe and elegant and . . . *odd*.

'Goodness, Cristina, you frightened me,' Claudia managed.

'I'm sorry, but I knew you wouldn't be in bed. I heard you come in.'

'Is something wrong?' Claudia slowly belted the silk cord around her waist.

'No.' Cristina paced a little aimlessly around the room, then suddenly she turned. 'Well, *yes*. I don't know how I can say this, Claudia, without sounding extremely interfering but I'm worried about you and Nick.'

It was so ridiculous Claudia laughed, albeit a shade hysterically. 'I suppose it makes a change!'

'Claudia,' Cristina said severely, 'I'm thirty-four years old. I've coped with failures, frustrations, my little triumphs, some defeats over a long period of time. You're just twenty-one and a very young twenty-one at that. You've led a very sheltered life. You've had little experience of the down turns in life.'

'I think all that has just begun to change,' Claudia said with a little flash of wry amusement. 'Why pick on tonight to give me a little ... sisterly advice?'

'As it happens I'm feeling very uneasy about you and Nick,' Cristina continued incredibly. 'I know he's been perfectly charming to you all these years but you were only an infant. You're a young woman now and very attractive in a virginal kind of way. That kind of thing appeals to a great many men.'

'You amaze me, Cristina,' Claudia said. 'Haven't you got enough of a problem without taking on mine?'

'For God's sake, Claudia. I'm concerned about you!' Cristina hit the back of a Louis XIV chair with a small, clenched fist. 'Nick Grey is far too much for you to handle. He could hurt you badly.'

'I'm well aware of that, Cristina,' Claudia said coolly, though her whole body seemed tied in knots. 'What would you have me do?'

'It's because you're so young, so inexperienced,' Cristina said. 'I have a duty to you.'

A duty? my foot, Claudia thought.

'So why don't we both tell Nick to go find his pleasures elsewhere?' she said grimly. 'By the way, Cristina, he has sworn to me that there is not and never has been anything between you.'

'And you *believe* him?' Cristina stabbed at her hair wearily.

'You told me the same thing yourself.'

'Then I probably will again.' Cristina's husky voice changed to bitterness. 'If I can't help myself, Claudia, I can help you. Nick is a strange man. Cruel. Maybe what he felt for me has passed but it left me with a lot of scars. Now he has turned his attention to you. You with the white-gold hair and big green eyes. Yesterday you were just a child he could help with your homework, today he's seeing you with new eyes. It could be something serious. I feel it.'

'Are you jealous, Cristina?' Claudia asked, not with any challenge but a gentle need to know.

'Does it matter?' Cristina's eyes momentarily filled with tears which she blinked furiously away. 'Maybe I am, a little. How could I not be? But more importantly I have a few decent feelings left. I want to protect you, Claudia. Give you the benefit of my painful experience.'

'Maybe none of us can do that,' Claudia said. 'Don't upset yourself, Cristina. I've never seen you cry.'

'Oh I *cry*!' Cristina said bleakly. 'I cry until my eyes are red and swollen.'

'So might we all after we get burnt. You went after Nick, Cristina. You can't deny that.'

'Yes, but he was so *provocative!*' Cristina put out an appealing hand. 'I'm used to men. I've been very much admired in my time, but I've never met anyone remotely like Nick.'

'He's not good husband material,' Claudia said.

'Oh, God, I know that of course.' Cristina stopped her pacing and collapsed into the Louis XIV chair looking very haggard but still glamorous. 'I'm scared rotten the man I *really* love might hear something.'

'I would be too,' Claudia couldn't resist saying. 'You don't *act* scared rotten, Cristina. Scared rotten ladies don't cling to other men in full view of their husbands.'

'Grant had his back to us,' Cristina said. She looked up her face white with indignation. 'Don't you go making trouble for me, Claudia.'

Claudia stroked her aching forehead. 'I weep for you, Cristina. I'm not out to make trouble.'

'Oh, I *know* that!' Cristina threw out a distracted hand. 'You're a good girl, so it makes it all the more intolerable to allow you to fall into Nick's clutches.'

'Oh, well, I have.'

'You don't *mean* that!' Cristina looked shocked out of her mind.

'If it makes you feel any better, I've been the same for the past eight years. I've always been gone on Nick, you know.'

Cristina stared at her stepdaughter for a moment, then laughed. 'But that was just a schoolgirl thing. I understand. We all have our crushes. I remember I was very taken with my maths teacher. In fact I could have taken him away from his wife but I was just a baby of sixteen or so.'

'Wasn't *he* lucky.'

'Look . . .' Cristina began.

It was imposible to be angry, only helpless and desolate. 'Please go back to bed, Cristina. I'm rather tired.'

'Did Nick make love to you?' Cristina asked, her eyes glowing strangely.

'As a general principle, Cristina, I think it's better *not* to kiss and tell.'

'He did, didn't he?' Cristina persisted.

'We can afford to,' Claudia pointed out sharply. 'He's not married and neither am I.'

'*Oooh!*' Cristina bent over like a woman in a wheelchair.

'I'm sorry if I've hurt you.' Instantly Claudia felt remorse. Cristina was obviously the victim of a powerful addiction. 'Why don't you go away for a little while, Cristina. You'll see things better. As they are. Daddy loves you and you've told me you really love him. That is as it should be. What you feel for Nick is some terrible fascination. It's unreal and *worse*, he doesn't *want* you.'

Cristina breathed in sharply her whitened face ghastly. 'How would *you* know?'

'I hope so, Cristina, for all our sakes.' Very fervently Claudia joined her hands. 'I know a lot of people don't seem to take their marriage vows very seriously, but Daddy does. If he heard *one* word about you and Nick, I think you'd be finished in his eyes. You see, my father has a thing about perfection. Women are sort of fantasy figures. All beautiful heroines. He could never tolerate second best. Surely you've seen what he's like? If you failed him I think he could cut you out of his life and never look back. He'd cut Nick out as well and terrible as it may seem he'd grieve more about Nick. Maybe I know my father better than you do. In *that* department I've a lot more experience. If you want your marriage and I know you do, you'll have to beat your feeling for Nick. Or grit your teeth and bear it. It will go away. Everything needs feeding. Even love.'

'Maybe I feel things more passionately than you,' Cristina said in a coldly cutting voice. 'You're a very cool, reserved sort of person so you wouldn't know. I came here tonight to make you listen to me. I can see from your face Nick made love to you. I'm far from being a stupid woman. You look turned inside out. You're supposed to be clever. If you are, take your own advice. Give Nick up. Let him go to that Amanda woman. She'll have him. With pleasure.'

'And *you* have?' Claudia couldn't let it alone, though she heard the same thing over and over. Nick had accused her of condemning him out of hand and she had to admit she had thought him highly principled for years.

'I'm one of the *unfortunate* ones,' Cristina said. She didn't meet Claudia's eyes but dragged herself to her feet. 'Forgive me for all this, Claudia. I couldn't just step aside complacently and allow Nick to have you. In the end, we're *family*.' Her thin, but well-shaped mouth twisted. 'I guess a year from now we can speak about this and laugh.'

'I don't think so,' Claudia said painfully. 'It's a terrible thing to see an idol fall.'

Cristina's jaw tightened but she said nothing. As she passed Claudia she put her hand on her shoulder, pressing down on it with the palm.

'I've said it all, dear, and I feel terrible, but I'm prepared to do anything at all to keep you and Nick apart. You're meant for better things.'

Claudia didn't answer. There was nothing to say.

CHAPTER FOUR

A FEW weeks went by of relative calm. They were all very much preoccupied with their own affairs. Claudia was preparing for her exams and concentrating intensely; Cristina had been asked to handle the renovation of the Ashleigh Hotel, a small hostelry that had seen grander days and Grant Ingram was totally absorbed in a very big commission, the Kuhn-Culver Building for which Nick was his chief designer.

'I don't know why I bother cooking at all,' Fergy complained. 'Never a day goes by that someone doesn't ring to say they won't be home.'

Eventually the week of examinations went past and Claudia was left face to face with the prospect of doing nothing. Of course it was coming in to the holiday season and even Marcus closed the gallery for a full month starting from Christmas Eve while he flew off to London, Paris, Rome, combining business and pleasure and making annual visits to his major, expatriate artists. At the end of her examinations Claudia had planned on a lovely long holiday at their beach house, maybe asking three or four of her girlfriends but now she felt too worried and nervous to leave the house.

'What *is* wrong with you?' Fergy asked one afternoon when Claudia was making an attempt to help her clean the impressive collection of silver that usually adorned the sideboard in the dining room. 'You seem awfully restless these days?'

'This is mine, you know,' Claudia said, polishing the magnificent tray that held a Victorian tea and coffee service.

'I know, dear,' Fergy said mildly. 'For that matter most of the silver belongs to you. By rights, that is. It was left to Miss Victoria by her grandmother who in turn had been given it by her grandmother. Valuable it is too, especially that Garrard tureen.'

'I like all the plain things best,' Claudia murmured, polishing absently, 'like that lovely little cup. Too much ornamentation doesn't appeal to me.'

'To say nothing of its being harder to clean.' Fergy, in fact, used a large, high quality paint brush to facilitate her cleaning of the richly decorated pieces. 'Why aren't you going to the beach as you said?'

'Don't feel like it at the moment.'

'Why are you avoiding Nick?' Fergy finally asked.

'Good Heavens, I'm not!' Claudia's voice held an urgency that gave her words the lie.

'*Why*, dear?' Fergy persisted. 'I really think it's going on a bit too long.'

'I can't explain, Fergy. It's very difficult.'

'I'm ready for it,' Fergy said rather dryly. 'Part of it is you're worried about your stepmother.'

'*Fergy!*' Claudia said helplessly.

Fergy turned her shrewd blue eyes directly on the girl. 'I've been around a long time, precious girl. You don't *really* think anything much escapes me?'

'What is it you mean?'

Wry little lines bracketed Fergy's mouth. 'My

eyesight mightn't be as good as it used to be but even then I've noticed Mrs Ingram finds our Nick *very* attractive.'

'How extraordinary!' Claudia said in that same distracted fashion.

'You mean that I noticed. How young you are, darling.'

'Cristina said the same. In fact, everyone says the same. How *young* you are, Claudia!'

'Who wouldn't turn back the clock!' Fergy sighed. 'Take no notice when your stepmother says it. Getting older is brutal for women. Some more than others.'

'Do you think Daddy's noticed?' Claudia asked fearfully.

'Not so far,' Fergy said. 'Your father has created a world of perfect order. Perhaps he doesn't *want* to see a flaw. Mind you, I wouldn't want to be your stepmother if she ever lets him down.'

'So what do we do?' Defeated herself, Claudia needed Fergy's support.

'About what, honey?' Fergy asked, smiling broadly. 'You don't think Nick is even vaguely attracted to your stepmother?'

Suddenly there was no support. No common knowledge. 'You don't think so, Fergy?' Claudia asked gravely.

'My dear, I don't think Nick likes your stepmother at all.'

'But he has always been charming to her.'

'As he is to everyone. Even *me*.'

'He really likes you, Fergy. You know that.'

'All right, he does.' Fergy smiled with pleasure. 'But what would you have him do, dear? He's very close to your father. In fact he's pretty well family. Not that his future would be at stake if he suddeny left the firm, but he owes your father a good deal. Brilliant or not it would have taken him a good deal longer to get where he is today. Another thing, your father hasn't a jealous, envious bone in his body. He's genuinely proud of Nick's great talents. He's even prepared to take second place which normally most men wouldn't do even for a son. Nick knows this. He's an orphan really, you know. He idolised his mother and she went off and left him . . .'

'There was no way she could *take* him,' Claudia pointed out defensively, 'and leave her husband.'

'Then she should have stayed with him,' Fergy said.

'I expect she felt terrible about it.'

'I don't condone her actions,' Fergy said. 'I remember her well. A glorious creature. Boyoboy was she beautiful! A female Nick.'

'How did she ever marry Nick's father?' Claudia asked. 'He's such a cold, remote man.'

'Basically I think he was just a very reserved, very sensitive person. It sounds so strange, I know when you think of him these days, but at the outset of their marriage no man could have been happier. He adored her. Worshipped her, if you like. But then she had a tremendous ability to *attract*.'

'Like Nick,' Claudia said very bleakly.

'Yes, like Nick,' Fergy was forced to agree. 'I don't know that it's an enviable gift. It's hard to lead an ordinary dull old life when you're immensely vibrant. Certain individuals have a powerful effect on others.'

'So you don't think Cristina's attraction is very serious?' Claudia tried to sound dispassionate.

'It would be *very* serious,' Fergy said sternly, 'if the attraction was mutual. I can't even dwell on it, but take it from me, sweetheart, Nick knows what he wants. *Who* he wants. There, isn't that a beautiful shine?'

The conversation should have reassured Claudia but it didn't. Shrewd and observant as Fergy was, her feeling for Nick and her underlying dislike of Cristina, for that was what it was, prevented her from seeing the truth. Nick was as guilty as ever Cristina was. Cristina wouldn't lie. One had only to look at her white, tormented face. Men were such absolute villains. They could lie beside one woman and tell her they loved her, then go off home and pretty well say the same thing. Other men even admired them for it. Maybe men had tremendously more powerful urges than women. Everyone said so. Fact or a darn good excuse.

Nick arrived one evening just as Claudia was waiting to go out. Fergy showed him in and they stood smiling, talking for a moment as Claudia came down the stairs. Immediately Nick looked up and Claudia wished to Heaven she knew what she could do to stop her heart from breaking.

'I'll leave you two to say hello,' Fergy said. Claudia had stopped dead on the stairs and even Nick had gone quiet.

'Daddy will be down in a few moments, Nick,' Claudia said politely. 'Won't you come into the library?'

'Where are you off to?' he asked, moving towards her, his eyes moving slowly down the

length of her body. She and Matthew were going
to a party and she was wearing a very pretty short
evening dress in a creamy, flower printed chiffon.
A thin, V-shaped halter caught the brief bodice
but the skirt billowed out from her small waist.
She wore her hair loose as well, but drawn away
from her face to the back of her head where it was
caught high by a silk rose. She looked beautiful
but somehow unhappy.

'Oh, just to a party,' she murmured, seemingly
as absorbed in staring at him as he was in staring
at her.

'You look like being beautiful doesn't make
you happy,' he said.

'I don't think beauty is supposed to bring
happiness. In human beings anyway.'

'Are you going to come down?' he asked, his
lean handsome face turning hawklike.

'Yes, of course.' She moved at once but he
stopped her when she was just a step above him
and almost on line with him.

'It seems to me you're getting positively
skinny.' His long fingers encircled her waist.

'You know what? I can't eat.'

'Really?' His eyes were so sparkling, so full of
light they were pure silver. 'Doesn't it make you
feel better I've mended my wicked ways?'

'Maybe it's because you're just too busy.'

'In fact I *don't* work twenty-four hours a day.
Twelve, maybe.'

'Daddy tells me the Kuhn-Culver is going to
be the best building in this city?'

'Including the Phillips we did last year.'

'Congratulations, Nick.' Her gentle voice was
bitter-sweet.

'Little bitch.'

'Once you would *never* have called me that.'

His hard, mocking face softened. 'I guess you're right,' he said coolly. 'Just as once *I* had your respect.'

'Sad isn't it?' She looked intensely into his wonderful face. Everything was so clean cut and definite; sharply drawn black brows, thick black lashes, fine grained olive skin tanned to a dark gold, straight nose, clean jaw, a mouth that caught the eye, shapely, expressive, the edges well defined.

'Surely you know what I look like, Claud,' he said dryly, his silver eyes glinting.

'I don't know what's in your heart.'

'But it's black and all that?'

'I can't joke about it, Nick.' His hands were still resting lightly about her waist but she couldn't seem to move for the life of her.

'Would you spend the day with me, Saturday?' he asked.

'Matthew wants me to go sailing with him.'

'Matthew tonight?'

'Yes.'

'Look at it this way, he's safe.'

'What does *that* mean?' Her green eyes flashed fire.

'He's been your close friend for just on two years.'

'You mean you've counted?' Her voice slipped into something of his own mockery.

'I have. Let's see. You're twenty-one now. I'm thirty-three. That's a lot better than thirteen and twenty-five.'

'God knows you *always* treat me that way.' She propelled herself off the stairs.

'*Always?*' He began to laugh.

The doorbell sounded and Claudia almost flew towards the door, ready indeed to charge into the night.

'Hi!' At the sight of her Matthew's smooth, good looking face lit up with admiration. 'You look like a poem!'

She *never* threw herself into his arms, but she did.

'You're right on time.'

'Hey, with this kind of reception, I'll never be late!' Laughing, excited, Matthew began to kiss her smooth cheek.

'*Claudia!*' Her father's resonant voice sounded vaguely scolding. He was standing on the stairs watching them, but Nick had turned away as if he didn't mind at all.

'How are you, Mr Ingram?' Matthew called respectfully.

'Fine, thank you, Matthew.' Grant Ingram came on down the stairs. 'Don't keep Claudia out too late tonight. She's a little tired-out whatever she says. All big eyes and fragile bones. She needs a good holiday after all that study.'

'I'll look after her, sir,' Matthew promised. 'I'd like to take her out sailing at the weekend. It'll be fun.'

'That depends on the weather, Matthew,' Grant Ingram said briefly. 'Excuse me now, I have work to attend to. Nick arrived, darling?' he asked his daughter.

'He's just gone into the library.'

'Good.' Instantly Grant Ingram's rather stern expression eased. 'You've left the phone number and address of where you're going?'

'It's Tiffany's place, Daddy.'

'Oh, Tiffany.' That apparently was all right. As he passed his daughter, Grant Ingram dropped a kiss on her forehead. 'Take care, darling. Remember, Matthew, you'll be *driving* home.'

'Yes, sir.'

'Struth!' Matthew breathed when they were safely outside. 'Is there ever going to be a guy good enough for your father?'

'For me, you mean?' Claudia smiled.

'I have the most dismal feeling your father doesn't aprove of me,' Matthew confided. 'Like I'm second rate.'

'Oh, Matthew, that's ridiculous!' Claudia reassured him. 'Daddy's like that with everyone. It's only sensible to know where your children are going.'

'Hang it all, Claudia, you're not a child. You're twenty-one.'

'A daughter is always a child to her father. I suppose it's part of father-love.'

'I guess your father is going to be one of those parents who tries to shape their daughter's life. Hasn't it ever struck you your father has your future husband lined up.'

'My father will allow me to choose for *myself*,' Claudia said a little hotly. 'Don't let Daddy's attitude upset you, Matthew. He's simply a caring parent.'

'Yes, and he doesn't care to see you with *me*.'

They had reached Matthew's car, now they stood almost glaring at one another.

'Are we going to a party or not?' All of a sudden Claudia felt like crying. She *was* run-down.

'I'm sorry, lovely one.' Matthew bent his head and very gently kissed her mouth. 'This isn't how I started out. I felt on top of the world. I'm crazy about you, Claudia, you know that. Sometimes I think you're my whole world. But then I come in contact with your father and I get worried. He's a very arrogant man. He really is. I know arrogant in a smooth, subtle way but arrogant all the same. No one and nothing challenges him. If you ask me, he's hoping and expecting you to marry Nick Grey.' This was said with a lot of hostility.

'Except that such a thing has never occurred to either of us,' Claudia retorted and her tone told Matthew to stop right there.

'Ah well, let's forget it.' Matthew held open the passenger door. 'Nick is years older than you and that makes a big difference. Especially when he likes the experienced sophisticates. All in all I don't think your father knows his beloved protégé at all.'

Because she had the time, and because her grandmother asked her to, Claudia found herself immersed in welfare work, and somehow or other although some of it was very upsetting it helped her considerably. Better still it was clear she was helping others. There were far more serious things in life to worry about than sexual intrigues. She was surrounded by people, men, women, children who were racked by bodily aches and pains; people who would remain in wheelchairs all their lives; little children who would never grow old. Most of all the children pierced her heart.

'You're very good with them,' Ward Sister told her.

'I'd like to be.' All she had done was sit and talk and because she had a facility for drawing elected to draw various favourite animals and cartoon characters. The children had been terribly impressed.

'Well done, Claudia,' her grandmother said to her, not in the least surprised. 'We must make good use of our time. Our lives are so comfortable but as you can see others are so wretched. We have a responsibility to help.'

Her father, however, was vaguely *annoyed*.

'Wherever are you off to today?' he turned to her one morning at breakfast.

'Meals on Wheels.' Claudia was gulping her coffee down so fast it was painful.

'Good God, can't somebody else do that? I really dislike your going into strange places.'

'But they're old people ... invalids, Daddy,' Claudia said incredulously. 'Nice, ordinary, decent people. Not so ordinary either. I met the most wonderful old lady the other day, gloriously strong in her mind but crippled with arthritis. She depends on us. Everyone *wants* to be independent, but it doesn't always happen. Especially when one grows old. I've seen so many people terribly afflicted yet they keep up good spirits. I don't know how, but they do. It's such a *lesson*!' The emotional tears welled up in her eyes causing Grant Ingram to cut in very curtly:

'This is your grandmother's idea!' he exploded. '*I* don't think you're strong enough. There are social workers for that kind of thing and they have the advantage of being *trained* which you definitely aren't. It's getting to you, my dear. Look at you now, eyes full of tears . . .'

Resolutely Claudia brushed them away. 'What I'm doing, Daddy, is extremely little, but since I've started, I'm going to keep at it.'

'For how long?' Grant Ingram asked sceptically. 'You can't eat and now you're shaking like a leaf. What *is* the matter?'

'Reaction,' Claudia answered after a moment's reflection. 'Reaction to seeing so much deprivation.'

'That's *it*! You're severely disturbed. Your grandmother has spent a lifetime in hospitals and such places. This is all too new to you.'

'Don't you think I can face it?' Claudia asked.

'You're very edgy, darling.'

'No. I'm just seeing a lot of terribly disturbing problems. It's a vast change from my usual day.'

'Ah well,' Grant Ingram turned back to his breakfast. 'Get it out of your system if you must. It seems a fairly morbid kind of work to me. Your grandmother never gets tired of all her charities but you're different. You'll kill yourself. As a family we contribute a good deal to charity. Surely that's enough?'

'I told you so!' Fergy wagged her head in the kitchen. 'Your dad's a real snob!'

'I don't think he thinks I can be trusted with such work,' Claudia said wryly.

'Because you're showing how much you *care* doesn't mean you can't do it,' Fergy said. 'You've got plenty of McKinlay blood in your veins.'

Claudia reminded herself of that when a pensioner she visited unloaded all her emotional difficulties on her as she served up the midday meal. The woman wasn't old but an invalid and although Claudia thoroughly understood her frustrations that particular case wasn't easy to deal with if it did add to her experience of crucial life. Because she listened, *really* listened, Claudia by the end of the fortnight had become very tired.

Because her grandfather was the person she found most supportive yet undemanding Claudia went over to spend her Saturday with him. He offered no advice, but allowed her to talk and as she talked she found herself dealing with her own reactions and adjustments. The treatment, in effect, was an open discussion and it proved very effective. Claudia made them both lunch and afterwards they worked together in the garden, giving one another tell-tale little smiles and pats that revealed very clearly where their deepest love lay. The loss of his daughter had been the most stunning blow Ross McKinlay had ever received in his life; a blow that drove him into deep depression, but suddenly—it was over. Looking into his granddaughter's eyes was not the reflection of pain but hope for the future.

They were sitting on the grass, quietly talking when the telephone rang. 'Shall I answer it?' Claudia brushed grass seeds from her hands.

'It's probably your grandmother. I'll go.' Ross McKinlay started to his feet, his eyes lighting up. 'Where that woman gets her energy from I'll never know. At an age when everyone else is slowing down, she's going at it full throttle. Like a cup of tea? It must be three.'

'Lovely!' Claudia swayed up very lazily and walked to the hammock strung between two gums. She felt so warm and relaxed she could drift off to sleep. Loving her grandfather so much it was like some marvellous gift to see him so much lighter in heart. His eyes had a glint in them and he had shared with her the latest news that he was resuming his old seat on the hospital board.

'Wonderful!' she had smiled and of course she had meant it. Later he had told her in a very business-like voice the changes he'd like to see brought about.

There was a smile in Claudia's eyes as she shut them. Was there ever a more delightful fragrance than newly mown grass? All the aching tensions seemed to have drained away from her body. She relaxed each limb in turn as her grandfather had long ago shown her . . .

'How about it, Sleeping Princess?'

Nick was looking down at her and she stared up at him in amazement. 'You *kissed* me.'

'I did.' His voice was both tender and jeering. 'Isn't that what I was supposed to do?'

She could feel her body temperature rising. 'It's a wonder I didn't cry out.'

'You did. A kind of little kitten mew. Can you get out of that or do you want me to lift you out?'

The hammock tipped suddenly and he seemed obliged to rescue her.

'Perhaps you could put me down, Nick?'

'Isn't there rather *less* of you?' he frowned. 'No, seriously, Claud, you'd better stop rushing around or you'll collapse.'

'Believe me, I'm perfectly fit.'

'Damn, you weigh nothing,' he said.

'Grandfather thinks I look all right and he's a *doctor*,' she protested. 'I insist you put me down.'

'I'm tired of holding you anyway.' He lowered her so she moved against him all the way. Her body reacted. So did his.

'Have you come to see Grandad?' she asked, a flush in her cheeks.

'I always like to see your grandfather. He's one of my favourite people, but actually I came to see you.'

'Did Fergy tell you where I was?'

'Why would she not?' he looked puzzled. 'There's definitely something wrong with you, Claudia. We've spent so much time together yet I was all wrong.'

'I know how it is.' She put up a hand and brushed her long hair from her face. She had never expected to see him today now her calm blood was glittering in her veins. 'Here's Grandad with afternoon tea!' she cried in relief.

'Just for survival, I think you need it.' He swung away from her and walked across the grass to where Sir Ross approached with a laden tray.

Grandad was such a marvellous judge of character, Claudia thought, he would hardly believe he had been mistaken about Nick. Now Nick had the tray and Sir Ross had his hand on the younger man's shoulder. Both tall, both handsome, both so desperately close to her heart. She could hardly tell Grandad of her fears. Grandad like her father thought the sun rose and set on Nick. From the beginning they had taken a particular interest in him, almost embracing him as family as they all knew his background and viewed his situation with sympathy. Rebecca Grey had walked out on her husband and young son and a few years later had been killed in a car accident. His father had turned into a cold recluse and his maternal grandfather, despite the fact he was elderly and plagued with ill health, had to emerge in the role of protector and guardian. Not that Nick had ever been disowned by his father, but as Claudia found out a long time after, his physical resemblance to his mother touched some raw nerve and kept father and son a good deal less close in their relationship. All in all, Nick had been deprived, but he had certainly found the answer to it.

'This is a nice surprise,' Sir Ross said. 'I asked Claudia how you were but she's seen as little of you as anyone else. They tell me the new building is going to be particularly good.'

Nick set the tray down on the white wrought iron table and Claudia drew up the chairs. 'I believe you've forgotten the milk, Grandad?'

'Damn it, so I have. Of course we drink it black.'

'I'll get it.'

'Sit down, Nick, and tell me all about it,' Sir Ross insisted. 'Grant dropped in the other night . . .'

The men talked on amiably for perhaps thirty minutes while Claudia inserted a comment here and there so they couldn't have it all to themselves entirely.

'I'd like to take Claudia out to see one of my houses,' Nick sat back in his chair and sighed contentedly. 'Please come with us.'

'I'd like to . . .' Sir Ross began then looked at his watch, staring at it in amazement. 'I believe thirty minutes in some people's company can just fly, and two minutes with others is too long. I'll have to make it another time. My darling wife is bringing home an unexpected dinner guest so I'll have to clean up the little mess I just made in the kitchen.'

'I'll do that, Grandad,' Claudia said, already stacking the cups, saucers and plates.

'No. Nobody understands how to stack our dishwasher except me.'

'Well, we'll carry it in anyway.' Nick took the tray.

'It's that Mrs Zimmerman,' Sir Ross chuckled. 'An excellent woman, but an horrendous bore!'

Nick smiled sympathetically. 'I know you'll be perfectly charming to her.'

'I should think so! I wouldn't like to see her generous donations to the hospital cut off.'

'It's great to see your grandfather in such good spirits,' Nick said as they drove away in the car.

'Yes,' Claudia agreed with gentle tenderness. 'It's been a long journey back, yet Daddy never mentions my mother.'

'We each deal with our wounds as we can.' Nick's voice was expressionless. 'I imagine, Claudia, he was desperately unhappy in the early days. Perhaps ready to go under. Your grandfather told me once life had no real meaning for him after your mother died yet he continued to care for others in the same way he had always done. Your father is a different kind of man. To keep going I think he had to seal the memory of your mother off completely. From time to time, before he met Cristina I used to see an expression of desolation flit across his face that he strained to stamp out. It couldn't have been easy, but he had his work.'

'A man always has his work,' Claudia said, rather bleakly. 'Grandad has never spoken about her either. Only Fergy and Nanna and they speak

about her, so naturally, she seems to come to life.
I *miss* my mother.'

'Yes, it's—hard.' Nick's taut face looked faintly
strained. 'I think a lot of us keep up emotional
barriers because of what we've missed.'

'Is that a dig at me?'

'Both of us maybe. I've never let any woman
come close to me. Only a little kid. One doesn't
throw up defences against little girls who look
like daffodils.'

'A little-sister figure, is that it?'

He flicked the briefest glance over her
summer-sheened skin. 'Never quite. There was
always too much promise of the beauty to come.
Besides, you've never thought of me as your big
brother?'

'No.' Even in her innocence she had sensed a
different element, a woman-thing through the
child.

'So here we are, Claudia, at what we've always
known.' He didn't speak again until they reached
the Devlin House, his expression faintly hostile
as though he had already confessed too much.
'We'll have to walk from here, Claudia,' he told
her as they came to the end of the unsealed road.
'The car's not built for bush tracks.'

'I'd *like* a walk.' Claudia was already opening
out the door. 'This is a beautiful block of land.'

'About ten acres in all. It looks away across the
valley. To some extent it was rather a difficult
commission. Mrs Devlin wanted a classic
Georgian, which wasn't on. Neither the climate
nor the environment. Professor Devlin wanted a
kind of American ranch. Dr Sinclair *told* them to
come to me much as Marcus tells his clients what

to buy. I think they were a little mystified by my designs, but prepared to try something new. The only thing they did agree on was, it had to impress their friends.'

'So you had to come up with something to suit the both of them?' she asked mockingly, knowing full well the answer.

'No. I designed a house that's at home in its site. Of course it had to relate to the people it served, but I can't have the clients telling *me* how to design a building. *I'm* supposed to be the expert. If they don't like my work they're naturally free to go to someone else but usually they come to me by deliberate choice. I just hear in essence what they want, but what the actual building looks like is up to me. There can't be totality if I'm playing off husband against wife, trying to strike a compromise or drawing too heavily on the past. My main concern is to find the appropriate expression for a building in a particular environment. As it happened my drawings struck a bell.'

'I'm not surprised.'

Nick's drawings were so brilliant, so beautifully washed in colour with all the phenomena of shade, shadow and light, they were already being collected as works of art in their own right. His drawing style was very personal and marvellously self assured; at once rich in information and distinctly painterly. Claudia's father's drawings were of a different type; diagrammatic, displaying his respect for symmetry and order, always traditionally orientated and elegant, but without Nick's extraordinary gift for manifesting the *actual* building. One could *walk* into Nick's drawings so vividly were they rendered. Some might find the concept too different or too daring for conservative taste but all understood the power of the intellect behind the conception. The people who actually lived in his houses, like Dr Sinclair, had undertaken to spread his reputation with the same vigour Nick had brought to designing their houses. Often he designed the furniture as well to the delight of the local craftsmen whose skills he sought to keep alive.

'What the heck's *that*?' she cried and clutched his arm.

'Oh, that? It's an ordinary old snake. Quite harmless. There's still quite a lot of clearing to be done.'

'Are there many more do you think?' She had moved so close to him he tucked her under his arm.

'Oh, come on, Claud. It's not as if it was a taipan.'

'You think it's silly, *I* don't. Snakes frighten the life out of me. Even the small fry and that looked about two metres long.'

'Harmless,' he said again. 'What are you doing tonight?'

'I'm staying at home.'

'How incredible!' He looked down at her, small in her flat sandals.

'Believe it or not, it's what I want to do.'

'How is Matthew?'

'Why?'

'I don't think you should encourage him as you're not in love with him.

'I don't have to be *told*, Nick,' she said. As a matter of fact she and Matthew had had rather a *scene* which was one reason she was staying at home that night. Matthew had been so nearly *vicious*, there was no other word for it, she still couldn't believe it. Always controllable in their light lovemaking he had become almost violent, justifying his actions by accusing her of being 'a precious little nun ... short on sensuality'. If only he knew! Or then again maybe his anger had been fed by jealousy because he had mentioned Nick a lot, with none of his old admiration but a whole lot of sarcastic innuendo.

'Possibly you've been overestimating your strength,' Nick said. 'Not many people, I think, have thrown themselves so hectically into community effort.'

'Okay, so Daddy's been talking?' She stopped and looked up at him.

'A little.' He looked tender and faintly amused. 'You're just the type to give yourself to a life of service.'

'Volunteers just happen to be *needed*.'

'I know that.' He pinched her chin and before she could stop him dropped a hard kiss on her mouth. 'It just happens I admire what you're doing, Claud. Don't *over-do* it, that's all. Even your grandmother started out with small doses and she's an enormously energetic lady. You get a very delicate look about you from time to time. You try *so* hard.'

'So would you, Nick ...' She let her voice trail off. Where he had kissed her, her mouth seemed to be flaming. It required so much effort to resist Nick and today resistance seemed to be entirely beyond her. Two giant royal poincianas were flaming on an adjoining property, resplendently scarlet against an enamel blue sky. Their massive limbs were motionless on the hot, still air.

'Are you ever going to design a house of your own, Nick?' she asked suddenly.

'Sure, baby.'

'What about your grandfather's place?'

'I've been thinking I could sell it to my cousin, Barbara, and her husband. They have *five* children!'

'Then it wouldn't go out of the family. He's a barrister, isn't he?'

'Yes.' He looked down at her, the darkness of his hair and skin the most extreme contrast with his eyes. Today he was wearing an open-necked soft shirt with casual slacks and she was acutely aware of his lean good looks. She even feared she might be staring. 'Come on, let's keep going,' he said.

The Devlin House rested on the pinnacle of the verdant hillside like its crowning glory, its multi-levels extending down the canyon, irregular expanses of glass affording viewing galleries for the magnificent 360° panoramas.

'But this is different to anything you've done before,' she said, just standing there, shading her eyes. It was beautiful. Brick, tile, rich red cedar, all commodities used time and time again but not like this. Nick's work was unmistakable, reaching out to one with its originality and scope. Thirty three, she thought. To have achieved so much!

'They're *all* different,' he said. 'An architect is always striving to create something new. I didn't want to frame all the views with the same old window walls. I approached it much as a painter does when he's thinking of appropriate frames.'

'This would be a wonderful place to live.' Claudia allowed herself to be drawn up the slope.

'I can do better.' His hand covered her shoulder and she understood for a moment it would be very difficult to get away from Nick if he wanted her. He was so determined she began to tremble.

'Stop that,' he said, knowing her too well.

The house wouldn't be ready for occupation for another month and there was no one around. Shadows were beginning to sweep the valley now and there was a curious magic in the air.

They walked around for a long time, Nick explaining what he wanted her to know, Claudia asking questions, her green eyes reflecting the haunting beauty of the valley. They seemed to talk unflaggingly, very naturally as they had not done in many long months. Many of her friends were desperately shy of starting up a conversation with Nick, thinking themselves somehow inadequate or lost for something really interesting to say to him yet she had always found Nick a very comfortable person to talk to . . . He didn't parade his brilliance or forever talk in profundities. He had always teased and amused her and so often been very, very kind. He was like that. Exciting *and* easy. For that afternoon she refused to allow anyone to come between them. There had been so much constraint between them now it was curiously like the old days.

'I guess we'd better be going,' Nick said eventually. 'In a little while it will be really dark.'

'Thank you, Nick. That was a marvellous experience.'

He shut the door and locked it. 'The

landscaping is going to be important, that's why I recommended Marc Adami. He'll clear it selectively. The trees are beautiful but we can't risk a bush fire. One can never be entirely sure in this climate. Precautions must be taken.'

Claudia picked up a white stone, smoothing it lovingly with her hand. 'I so envy you, Nick. If only *I* had a gift.'

'My God,' he said, 'you *haven't*?'

'I can do lots of things but nothing *really* well.'

'Keep trying, baby. You've just turned twenty-one.'

'Still,' she said, 'you've *always* known you were going to be an architect.'

'It *does* run in the family, flower-face.' He put out his hand and encircled her wrist. 'What is it you *want* to be?'

She looked at him and exhaled shakily. Less clear now were worldly ambitions. A breeze had blown up, flurrying through the leaves, sending up aromatic waves of perfume.

'Would it be so hard to be a wife and mother?' He was smiling at her and all of a sudden she felt the hot spring of tears. Hadn't she loved him all along? It was terrible, *terrible*! She wanted nothing more in this world than to have her love returned.

Pebbles rattled down the slope and she flew away from him, her head whirling. After such a beautiful languorous afternoon she was swept by a great frustration, a blaze of anger she found difficult to control. Nick was *not* as he seemed. He was full of contradictions and complications. As *she* was, yet she felt herself incapable of endangering the security of others' lives. Love was relentless but Nick didn't really love anyone. It was monstrous, but it was true. Why had she allowed herself to trust his look of tenderness and desire?

She put her foot down in a crumbling depression and abruptly went over, the wrench of pain making her sick and breathless.

'You crazy little fool!' he dropped to his knees beside her, his eyes on her whitened face. Somehow the violence of his tone implied a great concern.

'Yes, aren't I? she whispered honestly.

'Wait, don't talk.' He bent to examine her foot and ankle. 'God knows what you've done.'

'Shall I try standing up? The worst of the pain seems to be fading away.'

'Maybe you've only wrenched it,' he muttered. 'Only a woman could act in such a *hazardly* fashion.' He lifted her, doll-like, supporting her while she lowered her right foot gingerly to the ground.

'Well?' he gazed intently at her.

'Can you fix me up with a bed for the night?'

'Claudia, I can refuse you nothing.' The look in his eyes sent a shiver down her spine.

'Actually I think it's all right.' She was discovering to her relief that there was no sprain or something worse; probably a torn ligament, it was starting to swell.

'I think hot and cold towels will do the trick,' Nick said consideringly. 'They'll bring the swelling down at any rate. Then, I think, the treatment is to keep on the move. Keep the blood flowing.'

'Grandad will know.'

'*I'm* the doctor for tonight.'

'You've got that all wrong. I love your architecture; suspect your doctoring.'

'You could always hobble home.'

'From here? That would be terrible!' She smiled and looked up at him, all of a sudden totally dominated by his glance. 'But I've left my car at Grandad's!'

'Okay. So we'll ring and say we'll pick it up tomorrow.'

She sighed deeply, still troubled by her principles. The natural ease of the afternoon born of years of companionship had fallen back into the tension of the past months. Had Nick brought Cristina here with him? Had they embraced, kissed? Were they all driven by a power outside of them?

'What is it now?' he asked abruptly.

'I have to know something, Nick.' She slid her hand rather pleadingly down his arm.

His silver eyes glinted and the handsome mouth grimaced. '*Don't* mention Cristina.'

'But Nick . . .'

'I *mean* it.'

'Well, then, what is it you want from *me*?' she cried out, exasperated.

'As much as I can get.' He looked down at her very coolly.

'I can't get used to it.'

'For God's sake, you *can*!' He looked mocking and angry. 'You've had some kind of power over me since you were a beautiful little kid with a thick pigtail. I thought it was because I never had a little sister to love and spoil. My childhood wasn't so great. My father and I were worlds apart. My mother couldn't even spare me *your* deep sighs. There was no doting grandmother, no aunts. I suppose I was ready for you to take up a lot of room in my heart. You were so sweet and generous *then*. So sure I was hero material. Now you seem to have made your mind up very firmly that I'm quite without ethics. And once you've made up your mind, Claudia, you're relentless.'

'Oh, that's not *true!*' she lamented and because her ankle was hurting began to moan, 'oh, oh, oh,' very softly.

'How in hell did we start this?' he groaned. 'Here, let me carry you. You've gone rather white.'

No more use to think about it. She allowed him to lift her, her gratitude real. A woman was certainly inferior to the man in one respect: she couldn't match his physical strength. Didn't want to. Claudia turned her face into his neck and because the impulse was too fiery to be consumed, kissed it.

'Coming home with me?' the curtness of his tone had magically softened.

She nodded. Could he feel the *yearning* in her body?

'Fine.' His arms around her tightened and that way they made their way down the hill.

CHAPTER FIVE

By the time they arrived back at Nick's house it was already dusk and Claudia was experiencing a certain amount of pain and shock reaction. In fact she had begun to feel faintly disoriented as though some further misadventure were pending.

Nick's frown made vertical lines between his black, winged brows. 'You're in pain, aren't you?'

'Nothing very bad. I'm more light headed really.'

'Maybe I wasn't quite right to bring you. I can *call* a doctor,' Nick suggested.

Claudia gave her ankle another cursory examination. 'I only wrenched it so I don't think we need bother with that.'

'All right,' Nick said swiftly. 'Sit there until I come around to help you. It's only a short flight of steps to the house.'

They were parked in the huge garage that was not detached from the house but specially designed to blend in with the main building as an extra wing. They walked to the indoor staircase and when they reached the top of the flight of stairs, Claudia leant back against the timber railing while Nick hunted up his keys.

'Wait here a moment while I turn the lights on,' he told her.

'What are we going to have for dinner,' she asked gently.

'Let's thoroughly investigate that injury first. If there's the faintest chance . . .'

'It's *not* serious, Nick.'

'No, I don't think so,' Nick bent and inserted the key in the lock, 'but you still look a little shook up.' The lock turned and Nick pushed the door open. 'What the *hell*!'

'Oh, *Nick*!' Claudia underscored his tone of surprised alarm. '*Did* you leave the lights on?'

'Stay there,' he said, very definitely, his face tautening as he decided on a course of action. Many of his friends had sophisticated security systems to protect their property but neither he nor his grandfather had ever had the slightest trouble.

'Oh please, Nick, be careful!' Claudia warned him.

'I will be,' he moved into the kitchen preparing to search out a suitable weapon and as he did so, a woman's distressed voice called out:

'Is that *you*, Nick?'

'God almighty!' Nick stared back at Claudia, his handsome face stony.

'You'd better answer her.' To all outward appearances Claudia looked completely un-interested.

'*Answer* her!' Nick swore violently under his breath. 'What the hell is she doing here?'

'Your guess is as good as mine,' Claudia shrugged with bitter mockery.

'*Nick?*' The woman was walking towards them, her heels beating a tattoo on the parquet floor.

'And I'd decided to *believe* you from now on,' Claudia's voice sounded as though it belonged to somebody else. She wanted to sound angry, disgusted, vehement, but she only sounded spiritless and beaten.

Nick, on the other hand, was in a blazing fury. 'In here, Cristina,' he commanded.

Claudia closed her eyes. She thought of the last time she had seen Cristina rushing to Nick's side. She was a lot smarter this time: she would spare herself the pain.

'Oh, Nick, I'm so glad you're back!' Cristina's voice came with a rush of heartfelt gratitude but no hint of apology. It was obvious she was unaware of Claudia's presence on the outside landing.

'How the hell did you get in?' Nick countered.

'Why . . . the key!'

What else, Claudia thought wearily.

'You mean you *know* where to find a key to my house?'

'Why Nick, you sound so angry!' Cristina cried.

All anger had drained from Claudia. She felt ill. But if she expected Nick to let her go he all but yanked her inside.

'Claudia!' Cristina screeched.

'For Christ's sake!' Nick exploded, 'what goes on here? I figure you've got exactly two minutes, Cristina, to come up with an answer. After that, I'm going to fling you out my door and to hell with the consequences!'

'Would you like a lawyer, Cristina?' Claudia asked very formally.

'Sit down, Claud, and shut up,' Nick warned her with absolute menace even as he slipped a chair beneath her.

'I couldn't bear anything to happen now,' Cristina cried and grasped Nick's arm. 'I think Grant *suspects* something.'

'*Don't!*' Nick muttered with uncontrolled fury. 'Don't try me too far.'

'I knew it would come to this,' Claudia said in the same dull tone. 'God, what *fools* you are!'

'I'll use that against you, Claud, for the rest of your life.'

'Who cares!' Claudia hunched over in her chair. Trust Nick to sound so cold and wronged. 'I prayed this would never happen.'

'It never would except for that wretched Matthew,' Cristina shouted desperately.

'*Matthew?*' Both Claudia and Nick looked up with hard, questioning stares.

'What's *Matthew* got to do with this?' Claudia demanded.

'He's a trouble maker, of course,' Cristina snapped. 'I've yet to discover whether his interference was deliberate treachery or he just wanted to take a rise out of Grant.'

'Matthew would never do that,' Claudia said faintly.

'I would say he *would*.' Nick cut her off curtly. 'You must know he's crazy about you, Claudia, and I gather these days he doesn't like me. To tell the truth I always thought your friend, Matthew, a little strange.'

'You *amaze* me, Nick,' Claudia said.

'Come on, let's hear it,' he goaded her. 'Let's have some more of the moral censure.'

'Please *stop* it!' Cristina was shaken and appalled. 'Grant could be here at any minute.'

'Big deal!' Nick pulled himself away from the table. 'And just as well. I don't think I could stand any more of this.'

'This is how he *really* is, Cristina,' Claudia

fixed her stepmother with brooding eyes. 'You'd sacrifice my father, a good, decent, *faithful* man, for a man like *Nick*?'

'I was carried away.'

'You *lying* bitch!'

'I'm *not*!' Cristina turned to Nick with a pent-up violence. 'I did love you, Nick. *Madly*.'

'God you women are wicked creatures!' Nick shook his head, the twist to his beautiful mouth quite terrible. 'I think it's only men that keep you on the straight and narrow. Can't you see, Cristina, that you're taking my reputation away from me? That's a pretty serious thing. For instance you've got sweet little Claudia here believing in your story of tormented rape.'

'Perhaps it will help Claudia to keep away from you,' Cristina said.

As a remark it was disastrous because Nick lifted his hand and slapped Cristina sharply across the face. 'I'm not supposed to be a gentleman so do be careful, Mrs Ingram.'

'Oh, *Nick*!' Claudia burst out, appalled. Cristina's striking, sophisticated face was as red and crumped as a child's.

'Don't pity her,' Nick said, bitterly. 'She's a liar and a . . .'

'Nick, *please*!' Claudia protested, deeply shocked.

'There's only one way to get out of this,' Cristina said frantically. 'You must help me. *Both* of you.'

'Not *me*, lady.' Nick's handsome, high mettled face was implacable. 'I'm hoping your husband will toss you out.'

'*Claudia!*' Cristina wailed.

'Why should it be *me* to help you?' Claudia asked quietly. 'You've betrayed my father and——' broken my heart, she thought but didn't say.

'The trouble with you, Claudia,' Nick said frigidly, 'is you're still a half-witted adolescent. You're being manipulated by an unscrupulous madwoman, but you can't see it.'

'For God's sake, let's talk about this before something *happens*!' Cristina begged. 'I tell you Grant had a phone call . . .'

'From Matthew?' Claudia lifted distant, green eyes.

'From Matthew, the little rat!' Cristina confirmed, her wide mouth ugly with rage. 'I caught a little of what he was saying on the upstairs extension.'

'So you came *here*? Nick regarded her with his dazzling silver eyes.

'We have to *do* something, Nick!' Cristina moaned. She was wringing her hands together with increasing intensity, her skin pallid except for the dull glow on her right cheek.

'Make your plans if you must, but make them without me,' Nick told her indifferently. 'Claud, I think we should bathe that ankle.'

'If I didn't feel like weeping,' Claudia responded, 'I'd laugh.'

'What's going to happen now?' Cristina cried out with a touch of hysteria.

'Tell the truth for once,' Nick suggested with quiet violence. 'I thought you were a touch crazy, Cristina, but not poisonous. Yet here you are still lying in your teeth. That puzzles me.'

'I have some feeling for Claudia,' Cristina

protested emotionally. 'It's only natural I would want to protect her.'

'From *me*?'

Nick looked so peculiar Claudia snapped to her feet. 'Let's stop this *now*,' she grasped Nick's two arms. 'It seems the only *decent* thing you two can do now is spare my father unnecessary pain and humiliation.'

'I'll do that,' Nick returned coolly, 'if I can have *you*.'

'Claudia, don't listen to him! That's not the way.'

'What a brute you are, Nick,' Claudia said quietly.

'Yes, aren't I?' He put his arms around her waist and jerked her to him. 'And because I am what I am I'm going to have you by fair means or foul.'

'You leave her alone, Nick,' Cristina cried.

'Never.' Nick's light eyes were glittering like diamonds. 'I'll marry Claudia and you can go back to your husband.'

'What kind of solution is that?' Cristina laughed crazily.

'Oh, come, Cristina,' Nick said harshly, 'why would anyone bother to tell so many lies? Just to protect someone? I'd say the opposite was true. They write about this kind of thing in women's novels.'

'It must be a lot of drivel,' Claudia pressed her hands hard against Nick's chest, but he *wouldn't* let her go.

'You're such a swine, Nick!' Cristina said on a great wave of pain. 'Maybe I deserve this suffering, but Claudia doesn't.'

So engrossed were they in one another it took them many seconds to realise the front door bell was ringing incessantly.

'My God, it's Grant!' Cristina whispered, turning to a statue.

'Where the hell did you leave your car?' Nick took charge.

'I grabbed a taxi. It seemed better.'

'One day, my dear, you'll tell me how you got in.' Nick released the gulping Claudia and turned to the tall refrigerator. 'God bless you, Cristina, for coming. You're so happy for us. So happy!' While he was talking he was extracting a bottle of champagne from the inside of the refrigerator door, then reaching for glasses from a wall cabinet.

'What are you *doing*, Nick?' Claudia asked faintly in a voice of the doomed.

'Celebrating, darling. Don't be embarrassed. As soon as your father charges in, possibly waving a gun, I'm going to head him off by announcing news of our impending engagement.' Now he had popped the champagne cork and was pouring the wine into the glasses. 'I had no idea, Claudia, you could look so horrified.'

The front door bell pealed again. 'Choose a glass and bring it into the living room,' Nick ordered with no sweetness at all. 'Move, you idiots!'

'Oh, God!' Cristina wailed, reaching for a glass at the same time.

'It's very important we all act the part,' Nick told them. 'Cristina heard the news from you, Claud, and rushed over. I'd advise you both to pretend like hell. Don't worry about me. I'm already the radiant picture of a man in love.'

Nick moved away and they hurried after him, both in varying degrees of shock. Mercifully the slap mark on Cristina's cheek had faded and she was visibly making an effort to pull herself together.

'For God's sake, Nick, where *were* you?' They heard Grant Ingram boom.

'He could be *murderous*!' Cristina hissed. 'I'm frightfully important to him.'

'Why in blazes tell me now?' Claudia flung back at her, frightened now Nick might be in danger.

But no. When the two men entered the long, beautiful drawing room Nick was smiling, Grant Ingram was looking a little odd, but he had an affectionate arm wrapped around Nick's shoulders.

'Darling, what are *you* doing here?' Cristina almost flung herself at her husband. 'I mean it's all so sudden and romantic but hardly official.'

'*Daddy*.' For the life of her Claudia could give no more than a shaky smile.

'My little girl!' Grant Ingram extricated himself gently from his wife's impassioned clutches and moved towards his daughter. 'I'm so proud of you. So *proud*!'

For an instant Claudia felt like bursting into tears. Maybe it was a nice sort of feeling making a parent proud but was this how it was done? Getting engaged to Nick? Even had everything been perfect surely it was an odd way to put it? But essentially her father.

Claudia allowed herself to be kissed and blessed.

'Get a glass for Grant,' Nick instructed Cristina, a peculiar sparkle in his eyes.

'Of course.' Cristina took one look at him and hurried away.

'It was the oddest darned thing,' Grant Ingram told them afterwards, flashing them all an uncharacteristic humble glance. 'You know I actually thought——'

'*What*, Grant?' Nick leaned forward attentively, the very picture of integrity.

'Oh, hell what does it matter now?' Grant Ingram held up his champagne flute for a refill. 'Why should I mar such a wonderful occasion with unpleasantness.'

'Please tell us, Daddy?' Claudia pleaded gently.

'No, I'm damned if I will!' Grant Ingram laughed. 'Just a piece of mischief I should have disregarded in the first place. You can be quite sure there'll be no mention of it again. By the way, Cristina, where's your car?'

'She felt sure you'd find us out and you did.' Nick smiled at him. 'A taxi here and her husband to take her home.'

'This is what I've always wanted,' Grant Ingram said.

'Yes, it's *wonderful*!' Cristina seconded, wild-eyed. 'I know you'd love to stay, darling, but we're expected at the Fauldings' tonight.'

'Cancel it,' Grant Ingram said.

'No, don't do that, Daddy,' Claudia came to Cristina's assistance. 'They'll be so disappointed and we'll have our own big party, I'm sure.'

'We certainly will,' Grant Ingram put his arm around his daughter and kissed her. 'Thank you,' he said. 'You've never given me one moment's anxiety or displeasure.'

'I sound like a terrible bore.'

'Never, darling,' Grant Ingram said briskly. 'You're the *perfect* daughter.'

'There, didn't I tell you,' Nick drawled, after he had seen his visitors off, 'it went perfectly.'

'I don't think there can be any truth in the statement, we get what we deserve.'

'And all this time, you and your ankle!'

'If you look closely,' Claudia said tartly, 'you'll see that it's swollen.'

'Darling, I'm *sorry*.' For such a high-handed, autocratic person he did indeed look sorry.

'Don't touch me,' Claudia began to shrink away from his touch.

'Shut up. Does it hurt?'

'There's such a thing as being anaesthetised by shock.'

'All Cristina's fault,' Nick looked up at her, diamond-eyed. 'It will cost us both, this engagement, but fortunately we're all still alive. Your father was in a fury when he arrived.'

'Did Matthew really want to cause trouble?'

'He had to take his frustration out on someone.' Nick straightened, then lifted her. 'Hot and cold towels on this, I think.'

'Are you sure it's safe?'

'Cristina will act sensibly from now on.'

'Whereas I could go round the *bend* from now on.'

'I told you I was determined to have you,' Nick held her in his arms and looked down at her.

'Then let's agree on how long,' Claudia's green eyes were no longer wide and adoring. 'They say all any rotter needs is the love of a good woman, but I don't care for self sacrifice. This whole situation is disgusting.'

'Really I quite like it.'

All of a sudden she began to cry.

'Claud, don't. *Please* don't.' Nick lowered his dark head and nuzzled her cheek.

'It's all so disgraceful.'

He moved back in search of an armchair and found one. 'I've told you one *million* times I've never laid a finger on your wretched stepmother.'

Claudia only cried harder.

'She's really neurotic. I hope I'm not shocking you.' He lifted her tear-stained face and kissed it. 'You love me.'

'I do *not*!'

'Of course you do. You and I have had a real commitment for years.'

'That's good,' she mocked bitterly.

'Cristina is like a wounded animal. She continues to lash out in her pain.'

'Don't swallow *my* tears.' She tried to jerk her head away from his wandering mouth.

'Why not? I want every part of you. Under all that terrific lady-like cool is a lot of passion.'

She wavered a little at the intensity of his voice. 'I'm allowing this, Nick, for the good of my father.'

He laughed.

'Because it would kill him being made a fool of.'

'You know you have the most exquisite *skin*,' he ignored her.

'And you're an authority on a woman's skin,' she said nastily.

'Up!' His voice turned hard again. 'If you don't want a lover, I can practise some first-aid.'

'Be sure that's all I'm ever going to let you do.' Her heart ached dully in love and sorrow.

'Suppose you let *me* be the judge of that,' he returned coolly. 'Remember, a man with no scruples holds all the cards.'

It was a situation Claudia thought endlessly she could not accept, but wherever they went, their friends expressed a genuine delight. Some went so far as to say they had expected this all along. Even Sir Ross had sprung to life again immediately he heard the news.

'I couldn't be more happy for you, darling,' he had told his granddaughter, looking directly into her eyes. 'Nick is a fine man. Your love will keep growing.'

Claudia often thought her face would reflect her disillusionment, but the thoughts that transfixed her only succeeded in making her look dreamy, apparently the appropriate expression for a newly engaged girl.

The party was set for Christmas Eve. 'A combination of wonderful events!' as her father put it. She had passed her finals with flying colours, Christmas was such a beautiful time of the year and now the culmination of Grant Ingram's ambitions; the finest thing Claudia concluded she had ever done in her life was get herself engaged to Dominic Grey. If she didn't do another thing, she had justified her existence.

Cristina seemed to avoid her like the plague, working so hard at her business she had turned into an ultra-elegant wraith. Claudia was terrifed despair might be behind that frenzy of industry. Always a compassionate person Claudia felt the strong urge to try to make contact with her stepmother. The human condition involved

profound upheavals and the best man or woman
could be made vulnerable to a totally unacceptable
love affair; or so Claudia reasoned. What actually
happened between Cristina and Nick she did not
know. Cristina inferred a grand passion; Nick
denied *any* close relationship vehemently. Either
he was an appalling, practised liar or the victim of
a severe delusion. Wasn't love a madness? From
the very moment Cristina had met Nick she had
been in a state of high emotionalism; a state
uncommon to her and therefore more dangerous.

On that particular morning a few days before
her engagement party Claudia sought her stepmother out in her office.

There were a few people in the showroom
when Claudia arrived. George Nisbet, Cristina's
assistant, turned around to wave and smile at her
and Claudia returned the smile and continued
towards Cristina's office. Cristina was such a
clever woman and she deserved respect for all
that she had achieved through her own efforts.
Strange behaviour was not foreign to clever
people and clever women, in particular, had few
of their own sex to champion them. If they all
had to survive as a family, arriving at some sort of
harmony was crucial.

Cristina was seated at her desk with her head
down and Claudia crossed her fingers and spoke
out pleasantly,

'Hi! I hope I haven't caught you when you're
busy?'

In response Cristina jumped. 'Good Heavens,
Claudia, what are *you* doing here?'

This kind of reaction wasn't surprising, neither
was it reassuring. 'We see so little of each other

these days, Cristina,' Claudia said mildly, 'I thought you might come out to lunch with me.'

'Out of the question, dear,' Cristina returned firmly, and stretched her long neck to relax her throat muscles. 'Business is so hectic! You have no idea.'

'You've got terribly thin.'

'So I have!' Cristina stood up abruptly.

'Please talk to me, Cristina,' Claudia dropped into a chair.

'For God's sake, what about?'

'I *care* if you're unhappy.'

'And you want to make it clear *you're* deliriously happy?'

'I'm not.' Claudia was perturbed by the tension in her stepmother's face.

Cristina snorted violently. 'You should be.' She sat down again and fixed Claudia with challenging eyes. 'You've got yourself one hell of a man.'

'Are you still in love with him, Cristina?' Claudia asked sadly.

'I *detest* him!' Cristina gave a laugh that ended in a stifled sob. 'He betrayed me. Your father. Now, you.'

Claudia's face went white with worry and anxiety. 'Whatever was between you, Cristina, it's over. You've simply got to forget him.'

'How *can* I, when he's always under my nose?'

'I know.' Claudia shook her head helplessly. 'You need to get away. You and Daddy need a long trip.'

'Your father would sacrifice me for Nick any day.'

'What does *that* mean?' Claudia leaned across the desk and grasped Cristina's arm.

'You know your father idolises Nick. He's the son he has always wanted.'

'Why don't you give him one of his own?' Claudia suggested fiercely. 'It seems to me, Cristina, you're wallowing in unhappiness. If you want to save yourself, you'll have to determine on a course of action. You think Daddy is in raptures about Nick and me? Can you imagine what he'd be like if you fell pregnant? Gave him a son? The love Daddy has for Nick tells you everything about him. He's the sort of man who lives for family and heritage. He loves me, I know. He's been the best father in the world, but there has scarcely been a time when I wasn't aware a daughter is second best. The true heir, the person my father best relates to, is a son. When Nick came along he fulfilled that great need. There is an extraordinarily close bond between them. I suppose neither of them had anyone really meaningful in their lives.'

'How you downgrade yourself, Claudia,' Cristina said pityingly.

'Yes, don't I.' Claudia bent her platinum head. 'I am, in a way, a product of my environment. Daddy values me more for what beauty I have than brains.'

'You've got plenty of them too,' Cristina said quietly. 'Really, Claudia, I have to admit it, you're an extraordinarily nice girl. That's why I hate to see you make a terrible mistake. Believe me, you could never handle Nick.'

'It may not come to that,' Claudia clutched the side of the desk. 'You know why I took this step, Cristina. Why Nick engineered this engagement the way he did.'

'He wants you,' Cristina said bleakly, barely managing to keep the tears out of her eyes. 'Goddammit, you're *perfect*. You're beautiful, you're highly intelligent, and best of all, you're your father's daughter. What could be better for Nick?'

'Everyone keeps talking about *Nick*,' Claudia said resignedly. 'Does no one care about *me*? What *I* want?'

'But you love him, don't you, dear?' Cristina put a beringed hand to her temple as though to stop the jabbing pain there. 'You'd be lying if you said you didn't.'

'To have him love me would be much better.'

'I don't think any woman is going to have Nick's *love*.' Cristina murmured huskily. 'He's got so many hangups deeply buried within him. He used to talk to me about his mother . . .'

'*Nick* did?' Claudia frowned.

'Of course.' Cristina seemed lost in her reflections. 'I think that's why he is such a bastard to all women. He's got the power now to destroy the sex he really despises. She went off and left him, you know.'

'Of course I know,' Claudia's green eyes searched her stepmother's. There was something about Cristina's expression that was really odd. A kind of theatricality but then theatricality was part of her makeup. Even part of her job.

'I don't believe Nick said too much about his mother,' Claudia said with a very sceptical air. 'Did he mention Valentina?'

Cristina smiled. 'I know all about Valentina.'

'That's odd, since I just made her up.' It was extraordinarily exhilarating to catch Cristina out on just one little lie. People who habitually told little lies inevitably worked their way up to the humdingers.

'Maybe it wasn't Valentina,' Cristina shrugged. 'I can't remember all the names but what I'm telling you stands. There's a lot of violence in Nick. A lot of hostility against women. Maybe that's what makes him so terribly attractive. Women love to be hated.'

'I'm afraid I can't agree with that.'

Cristina eyed Claudia's youthful beauty contemptuously. 'You're just a child as far as I'm concerned. Nick told me the same thing. You're the virginal little girl-child.'

'That's nothing to be ashamed of,' Claudia returned tartly. 'So long as I don't remain a virgin forever, I don't mind.'

'Don't turn yourself over to Nick,' Cristina advised harshly. 'He has a heart of glass. Look at how callously he treated me. Amanda Nichols was another one caught in his web. He takes what he wants, then he can't even remember. Men are like that.'

As an attempt at reconciliation it was quite unsuccessful. Cristina's sickness was even worse than Claudia suspected. Everything she had hoped for so *stupidly* was not to be. When an obsession took root it was hard to tear it up.

Claudia was just emerging from a department store when someone touched her on the arm.

'Claudia?'

It was Matthew and Claudia's soft, moulded mouth tightened. 'Oh, it's you, Matthew.'

'Oh, don't be like that, Claudia,' Matthew

begged in a husky voice. 'Look, have you time for coffee?'

'Not really, *no*.'

'*Please*, Claudia. Won't you let me explain?' Matthew's lean hand came out and tightened around her wrist. 'Just ten minutes? We've been friends for so long.'

Claudia wanted to say no, but Matthew was almost dragging her away. 'Don't keep on judging me, Claudia. I hated what I did but I wanted to show Nick up.'

'Then you made a big mistake, didn't you?'

The lunch time crowd had almost moved out and they found a table close to the floor to ceiling glass walls where they could look out at the people moving through the mall.

'You look beautiful, Claudia,' A muscle jerked beside Matthew's attractive mouth.

'I feel fine.'

'Being engaged must agree with you?'

'I didn't come to discuss my engagement, Matt,' Claudia stared rather numbly at the magnificent emerald flanked by diamonds on her left hand.

'Oh God, oh God,' Matthew said huskily. 'You could have anyone you please, Claudia, but not Nick Grey.'

'Why not?' Claudia was trembling inside but on the outside she was porcelain cool.

'Oh, please, Claudia, don't make me say it. Nick goes back a long way. You're just an innocent young girl. You don't know what you're getting into.'

'You know this is funny in a way,' Claudia laughed oddly. 'Everyone wanting to put me off Nick.'

'*Everyone?*' Matthew queried sharply. 'I thought *everyone* was thrilled to bits. All I seem to hear is the wonderful news.'

'I love him, Matthew.' Claudia took a deep breath.

'Then God help you.' Matthew's voice was as harsh as hers was soft. 'How can this have a happy ending after what Nick has done?'

'What *has* he done?'

'Don't let's go over that again,' Matthew drawled, his voice dripping acid. 'What kind of man would get involved with a close friend's wife?'

'Simple. He's been damned by a whole lot of circumstantial evidence.'

'You don't believe that?' Matthew challenged her.

'Maybe I do when the opposite is being rammed down my throat. Maybe I should be bitterly ashamed of myself for ever doubting Nick for a moment. Too many people are trying to convince me he *is* what I *know* he isn't. Nick may generate a lot of magnetism but he's much too unconscious of it to use it in the way you say. Other people make fools of themselves over Nick, but really he always remains the same. I used to think you liked him, Matthew?'

'I *did* like him.' Matthew hadn't taken his eyes off her lovely face. 'But having your girl taken off you is a nightmare.'

'Oh, Matthew,' she whispered, seeing his mouth twist in pain, 'I'm sorry. *Very* sorry, but I was never your girl. We were friends, good friends. I trusted you.'

'Your father did his best to cut me out,'

Matthew said viciously. 'I was never good
enough for you. Or him.'

'That's not true. But does it matter now?'

'You haven't walked up the altar yet, Miss
Ingram,' Matthew said grimly and caught her
hand. 'I've made my decision and that's to stick
around. You really matter to me. Grey may have
convinced you he loves you and maybe he does.
For *now*. He's the type that finds it impossible to
resist a beautiful girl.'

'*Rubbish!*' At least Claudia could deny that
emphatically because it simply wasn't true. Nick
had been known to resist any number of
glamorous girls.

'You know he's had that affair with your
stepmother.'

'I know nothing of the kind.' Claudia's eyes
were brilliantly angry. 'No matter what *you* tell
me. No matter what anyone tells me, I should
know Nick.'

'You mean you *do* know. Not *should* know. You
don't know, do you Claudia?' Matthew shook his
head. 'You're really under a great deal of tension.
Don't worry, I feel for you. The pressure must
be enormous. Wondering whether your father
really will find out. Whether Cristina and Nick
will get together again?'

Claudia's anger fizzled abruptly. 'What do you
think *caring* really means, Matthew?'

'I *love* you.' Matthew leaned forward and put
his hand over hers.

'I always imagined caring means being protective. You deliberately tried to hurt my father . . .'

'And I'd try again.'

'And in hurting my father you must hurt me.'

'So there was no way to avoid it,' Matthew's voice was anguished now. 'My life is worth nothing without you. I've gone mad since you got engaged.'

'Is that what love is, *madness*?' Claudia was struggling to wrench her hand away. 'People who are usually so sane and sensible overwhelmed by delirium. It's almost like a *disease*, not a happy event.'

'It's only happy when it's *returned*.' Matthew still held her fingers defiantly. 'Haven't you ever been *jealous* of anyone, Claudia?'

'I must have led a very narrow life. No, I've never experienced that unhappy, destructive feeling. I don't like *threatening* anyone anyway. I suppose I don't see things only in terms of myself. Finally, I guess, I'm not the smouldering type. Jealous people can be horribly wounding to others as well as themselves. You had no right to try to cause trouble, Matthew. I can't think why you did it.'

'You just told me,' Matthew laughed grimly. 'I can't take this relationship of yours with Nick Grey. I sure as hell can't. If there's anything I can do to stop it, I will.'

At the look in Matthew's eyes Claudia felt her skin go cold. She jerked herself to her feet and grasped her handbag.

'Don't go, Claudia. Please, *don't*.'

She shook her head. 'Our being good friends didn't mean a thing, did it, Matt? I think you're interfering because you enjoy it.'

'No, it's more serious than that,' Matthew looked up at her. 'You're *my* girl. At least I always thought of you as that. Nick Grey's got a lot of things going for him, I'll admit, but he's like the rest of us. He can't take a stab in the back. Your father is so wrapped up in his own life, the good life, he can't see what's right under his nose. One learns quite quickly to play dirty.'

'And some of us never learn at all,' Claudia gave him a look that was a mixture of disgust and sorrow. 'Before you start to think of attacking Nick or my father, remember they're both powerful men. And on the subject of your finding a plush job in the near future you're in the same field. My father has always stood for the Establishment. Nick is an establishment on his own. Both of them are kind of hero-figures. You just could shatter your own future.'

But Matthew was determined to have the last word. He noted the paleness of Claudia's flawless skin, the faint tremble in her hands. 'Better mine than yours,' he muttered. 'You must learn how to be your own person, Claudia. Up until now you've been manipulated by two men. That's all you're good for.'

'In that case then, Matthew,' Claudia said gently, 'I'm not the woman you want.'

CHAPTER SIX

THE festive season came and went and Claudia had to act radiantly happy all the time. She supposed the same was true of Nick. No matter how they felt they both had to go out of their way to be convincing as a couple very much in love. It was a classic love story really. So many people professed to know it was a relationship that was inevitable.

'No wonder he never took any of us seriously,' Amanda Nichols told Claudia with pursed lips. 'I said all along he was simply in love with somebody else.'

It was intolerable and all the private agonising changed nothing. Cristina had become a changed woman, finding fault with everyone and everything.

'If she speaks to me just one more time,' Fergy threatened grimly.

Finally Grant Ingram thought it was time to speak to his daughter. He had returned from a business meeting in high spirits, another important commission and the preliminary talks had gone well, but these days his wife wasn't treating him with the same attention and respect. Once she had been marvellous, glowing company, now she was strained beyond belief.

Grant Ingram walked downstairs again, trying to come to terms with the extraordinary difference in his wife. He had always thought Cristina remarkably consistent for a woman, but now her moods swung alarmingly, taking the form of extreme irritability in most cases. She was clearly in need of a holiday but he simply couldn't spare the time. In reality he detested any threat to the smooth pattern of his existence and whatever emotions had been involved when he made his decision to marry Cristina, love hadn't been one of them. He had only loved once and that had turned out disastrously. Besides, the older a man got the less likely he was to fall in love madly. Such stressful emotions were for the young. He had married Cristina because it had seemed an excellent idea at the time. She was highly attractive and clearly able to stand on her own two feet; they worked in a complementary environment and during those early days his friends had been very impressed with her. Now everything seemed to have changed and the general feeling was one of having made some huge mistake.

His daughter was in the living room waiting for Nick. They had tickets to a concert, a visiting concert pianist, and Claudia looked up at him with loving, trustful eyes.

'Downstairs again so early?'

'I love you very much, Claudia,' her father stared at her. 'You always behave so *well*.'

'Someone you know doesn't?'

'Pour me a whisky would you, darling?' Grant Ingram asked thoughtfully. 'I'm worried about Cristina. She's not well.'

'She's been working too hard.'

Grant Ingram frowned and looked at the floor. 'Dash it all, she's had two weeks' break.'

'Not enough,' Claudia murmured, holding out the crystal tumbler.

Her father took it without looking at her, his elegant, handsome features quite grim. 'You know what she just said to me now?'

'Isn't that a little private?' Claudia touched her father's hand appealingly. 'Can't you both go away for a holiday?'

'I'm darned sure *I* can't.' Grant Ingram looked outraged at the suggestion. 'Besides, I don't think a holiday would make Cristina happy. There's something deeply troubling her.'

'Maybe.' Claudia glanced away.

'Any idea what it could be?'

'Not really,' Claudia laughed a little shakily. 'We women are emotional creatures.'

'I don't really like it.'

'Of course. But Cristina mightn't like it either.'

'It's quite unfathomable to me.' Grant Ingram chose to ignore the faint irony in his daughter's musical voice. 'In my opinion she needs help. Maybe it's a *physical* thing that's causing the change in her behaviour. Women are such biological mysteries.'

'My suggestion is a *holiday*,' Claudia answered very seriously. 'Can't you manage even a *short* time together. Just the two of you. Maybe Cristina feels she has to share you with too many people.'

'Do you think so?'

'You're never really alone, Daddy,' Claudia said.

'Surely she doesn't want me to send *you* away?' Grant Ingram asked incredulously. 'And another thing, she's very nearly poisonous to Nick.'

'She *is* rather offhand,' Claudia moved away and her thick, beautiful hair swung bell-like at her slender shoulders. In the last months she had somehow matured, the soft, dewy look of girlhood refining to a startling beauty. Always, underneath ran worry.

'That's a very kind word for it,' her father said acidly. 'Would you believe that ex-friend of yours, Matthew, inferred there was some particular ... *friendship* between Cristina and Nick.'

'How very odd!' Claudia flung back carelessly, shaking inside.

'Damned odd!' Grant Ingram's handsome face turned fierce. 'I never liked that boy. Underhand.'

'Maybe foolish like everyone else at some time.'

'Really?' Her father raised a sardonic eyebrow. 'I assure you, my darling, I've never been involved in any messy intrigue.'

'I know.' Claudia sank deeply into her armchair. Her father was such a fastidious man and she had to admit very self-centred really. Still, out of her love for him, there was the fierce need to protect him.

'Privately, you know,' Grant Ingram confessed, 'I never thought Nick approved of my choice of Cristina for a wife.'

'Nick would find fault with anyone.'

'Now *that's* an extremely odd thing to say.'

'I was joking.' Claudia sat up and smiled.

'Yes, you were joking,' Grant Ingram looked at his daughter very searchingly. 'When are you and Nick going to set the date?'

'Gosh, Daddy,' Claudia's huge, green eyes

glittered, 'we've just had an engagement party. How can you possibly face a *wedding* so soon?'

'I'd go mad only for you and Nick,' Grant Ingram said very calmly and slowly. 'My life isn't so perfect as it seems. Sometimes I think it's a complete fabrication.'

'Daddy.' Claudia flew up and went to her father. He seldom, if ever, spoke this way. 'I know things are a little difficult at the moment, but they'll come right.'

'What *is* wrong with her?' For once Grant Ingram sounded bewildered.

'Down periods are part of life. Maybe Cristina doesn't recognise her limits. With you for an example she works exceptionally hard. Relaxation is valuable to keep people on an even keel. Why don't you go upstairs and tell her you're taking her to San Francisco for a week and no arguments.'

'I really can't spare the time, darling,' Grant Ingram murmured rather miserably.

'Nick will hold the fort.' The intensity of Claudia's expression betrayed her own urgency.

'Claudia, listen,' Grant Ingram suddenly said. 'There *was* never, could *never* have been any special relationship between Nick and Cristina?'

'*Daddy!*' Claudia looked and sounded appallingly shocked.

'I'm sorry, darling, but I'm serious. Terribly serious.'

'Because Matt put some incredible notion into your head?'

'Because of the big shift in my wife's behaviour.' Her father murmured, his voice low.

'Nick loves *me*,' Claudia said, her slender hands trembling.

'God, don't we all know it!' Grant Ingram seconded emphatically. 'Every time his eyes touch on you they give him away.'

'Then there's your answer, Daddy,' Claudia put out her hand and very gently touched her father's cheek. 'What you're saying is unthinkable.'

'I know it is.' Grant Ingram held his daughter's hand and kissed it. 'Thank you, dear. I didn't want to say that but somehow I felt forced into it. That's the rotten thing about gossip, innuendo. It stays in your mind.'

When Nick arrived her father was his confident self again, smiling on them both with a special warmth. 'I've asked Claudia when you're going to set the date?' he challenged Nick smilingly.

'And what did she say?' Nick asked faintly dryly.

'She's not at all over the engagement.'

'Then I'll have to persuade her she belongs by my side.'

Outside under the starlight she laughed a little wildly. 'How long are we going to go on like this?'

'Until we've got nothing better to do.' Nick opened up the car door for her.

'I don't think you know what life's like at our place.'

'Yes I do,' Nick returned, very curtly and distinctly. 'Get in, Claudia, for God's sake.'

She told her about her conversation with her father and he listened without comment.

'I'm frightened, Nick.'

'Why not? This is Saturday night.' Expertly he dodged a small sedan that came around a corner at him, unaware.

'Are you *ever* serious?'

'I thought you preferred me this way.' It was an acid comment on the state of affairs that existed between them. Far from acting like a lover, in the past weeks Nick had scarcely touched her.

'I'm afraid Cristina might crack up.'

'But not before the rest of us do. Fantasising must be your stepmother's only reality. You seem to shrink from a show-down but I think your father is strong enough to take it.'

'That you're not *perfect*!' Claudia cried.

'Do be careful,' Nick suggested. 'I know you have absolutely no faith in my honour and decency so I've nothing to lose.'

'I'm doing this very badly.' Claudia turned her face and looked out the window.

'Yes, you are,' he agreed bluntly. 'I can't feel sorry for Cristina, my darling. So far as I'm concerned Cristina is a crashing bore. Perhaps your father would be well rid of her. Perhaps she would be far happier if she moved house. Life is short enough, God knows, without making it a misery. The worst thing *I* ever did to your stepmother was to say hello to her. Someone should have explained to me she has a problem. More goes on inside her head than in real life. Or it's natural to a woman to create chaos out of nothing. Certainly she doesn't mind lying.'

'For what reason?' Claudia asked, her eyes filling with tears.

'Well, she sure doesn't want to see you with me. Not because, my angel, I'm a bad influence, but because she's had an absolutely, glorious crush on a man who doesn't want her. It's very,

very crazy, I'll admit. But then I venture to say, a lot of women *are* downright crazy. I've already begun to have my doubts about you.'

His effrontery fairly took her breath away.

They parked the car without difficulty and walked the short distance to the concert hall where they immediately encountered friends.

So here it is again, Claudia thought, hastily rearranging her expression. The prospect of any kind of settlement seemed a long way off. It was in a helpless mood she took her seat but when Nick told her beneath his breath to snap out of it she expelled a little sigh and tried to compose herself for enjoyment. The concert hall was packed and now as the soloist walked out on to the stage, the waves of enthusiastic clapping broke out.

'Do try to enjoy it, darling,' Nick drawled mockingly and squeezed her hand.

But somehow she could not. The music entered into her, overwhelming her with its power but even the chosen programme was full of passion and poignancy. After the interval there was respite with some Mozart of shining tranquillity, but then the soloist went back to oceanic turbulence, arousing the entire audience to an emotional response.

Not even the encores were frivolous.

'Absolutely marvellous!' Nick said sincerely. 'Let's get away from here now, before the crowd.'

'Did you keep the programme?'

'I've got it.' He glanced down at her for a moment, her soft lips apart. 'You shouldn't be so beautiful, Claudia.'

'You're frowning.'

'I'm not exactly a happy man.' He held her arm as they plunged through the crowd and the touch of his hand on her bare skin was an exquisite agony. Without speaking, there was no *need* to speak, a rising desire was between them. It was a paradox of her feeling for him that even as she burned at his touch, she could weep for her own weakness. His power over her was daunting and her sudden resistance may have accounted for the swiftness with which she broke away from him. The city gleamed around them, the street filled now with a confusing spill of people and the car not very far away. There was no good reason for what she was doing, indeed it was ridiculous but the evening of music had increased her feeling of emotional strain.

As she stepped out from the kerb, someone shouted and as Claudia looked up she was seized with dizziness. A late model Mercedes was moving at speed, running the amber light, but even as she was assailed by a weird paralysis she was caught up from behind and half lifted, half-dragged back to safety where she almost fell to her knees.

'Struth, that was close!' someone breathed.

'Claudia, are you all right?' Nick asked, his features so tight his face looked like a mask.

'That fellow should have been arrested,' an elderly man's voice said. 'Ah, there's a patrol car going after him.'

'It was my fault,' Claudia started to say. She and the Mercedes driver had both jumped signals.

'All right, miss?'

Nick whirled around as a constable approached them. He was young with a smooth, regular face yet he possessed an air of authority. 'Mercifully, yes, officer,' Nick said.

A small crowd was standing around and Claudia felt very stupid and exposed. Finally it was all over with a small lecture and Nick was leading her away.

'That was the closest I ever got to being run over,' Claudia managed shakily.

Nick was too deeply in thought to answer.

'Are you angry with me, Nick?' she asked uneasily as they drove away.

'I am angry, thank you.'

'Look, I've ruined my stocking.'

'Lucky, aren't you?'

'That was a great stunt saving me.' She tried to laugh but it wobbled a bit. 'Thank you, Nick. You always were very fast on your feet.'

'A whole fraction of a second to spare.'

'This is wild,' she threw her head back. 'You're *hostile* because you saved me from injury.'

'There is an element of hostility, yes,' Nick agreed with hooded eyes. 'What were you thinking about, Claud, when you pushed out in front of a moving car?'

'Truly, I never *saw it*.'

'So you're *not* self-destructive?'

'It was just a stupid thing to do. Gosh, the green light came on a half second later.'

'I'll have to take that into consideration.'

'You know what? I wasn't even scared. Just paralysed.'

'Well, I was scared out of my wits,' Nick returned very curtly. 'One minute you were there beside me, the next you're streaking under a car as fast as your legs could carry you. If you can't

stand thinking of me as a fiancé, try to think of
me as an old friend.'

'My dearest friend, one time, I might add.'

His silver eyes glanced briefly at her vulnerable
face. 'And your future husband, by God!'

'How fierce you are!' She responded to an
intensity that was almost alarming.

'Just so long as you know what you're up
against.'

This was determination of a kind Claudia had
only read about in books. She was conscious of
her thudding heart and Nick's fine, lean hands
upon the wheel. It seemed an eternity since he
had touched her.

'Do you remember that time I fell off the
swing?' she asked, old memories coming together
and meshing.

'Perfectly,' he said dryly. 'I damned nearly
kissed you.'

'But you *did* kiss me.' She turned her head to
look at his chiselled profile.

'I *did* not. As I recall I pecked your forehead. I
meant really kissed you. It was just as well there
were about twelve other people around.'

'My God!' she said gently. It had been a tennis
party and she had gone to cool off on her old
childhood swing. She saw in her mind the tall,
green trees, their group of friends and beyond the
tennis court where her father was playing with
dazzling prowess. Someone had pushed her off
but within a few minutes one of the chains broke
and she was thrown in an arc to the ground where
she lay still in winded misery. Nick had reached
her first. He had taken her into his arms. Then.

'It was the first time I saw you on your back in

the grass looking up at me. I don't know what I read in your face but I knew there and then you were no longer a child.'

'I was sixteen.'

'*Would* you have let me kiss you?'

'Yes.' Excitement fluttered in her stomach. 'Please don't go home, Nick,' she whispered.

'Your home or mine?'

'I mean . . .'

'*Tell* me. I really want to know.' His voice was crisp and quite devoid of expression.

'I want to be with you.'

'You mean you can't stand it any longer.'

'*Nick* . . .'

'Obviously getting around to telling me you love me is going to be very, very painful.'

The city had retreated and they were into the garden suburbs with a silvery moon cutting straight down through the hills and illuminating the valley like a stage. 'But you *are* going to your place,' she said.

'Of course I am.' He put out his left hand and brushed her hair from her cheek. 'I think I've held out for an indecent length of time.'

The heat of desire shimmered in her veins, flushing her creamy skin. She knew he was looking at her but she couldn't find the strength to resist temptation. She ached for him. Heart and body and soul.

'Darling, I won't seduce you,' he said very gently. 'Or as far as I'm able. God knows you've been a high risk for a long time now.'

'Do you always like something dangerous, Nick?'

'Do *you* know what trust means?'

She turned her face away from his while the trees and houses went by in a blur. Nick was the embodiment of excitement and she knew in her bones she had surrendered long ago.

Another few minutes and what everyone called 'the old Somerville place' was before them. The headlights picked up trees and shrubs and splashes of colour. It was almost a woodland and then the house. The garage doors were operated by remote control but tonight Nick chose to leave the Jaguar in the circular drive.

'You chose to come, Claudia,' he told her as they walked towards the front door.

'So?' She lifted a scarcely composed face to him.

'You look like you can't handle it. You look ready to cry.'

'I'm really sorry. You're used to more experienced women.'

It was a while before he spoke again, pausing at the bottom of the stone stairs flanked by a pair of terracotta Pharoah dogs. 'That was really silly, Claud,' he said, pushing aside a thick profusion of ferns.

'I'd be quite happy if you wanted to do a bit of gardening.'

'Actually I'm looking for a spare front door key. Your dear stepmother found it so I guess *I* can. Grandfather always left it here so as to be sure neither of us ever locked ourselves out.'

'Would you like help?'

'No, thanks. I have to take it slowly in the dark. Aaah, here it is.'

'Wow! You must be feeling very pleased with yourself?' Claudia couldn't remember ever sounding so brittle and mocking before.

'Let's go in, shall we?' Nick invited. 'I thought your father was the only one to know but evidently I should have pledged him to secrecy.'

'I'm still considering the insult to my deductive powers.'

'Easily explainable things are the most likely, you know.' His hand had gone to her wrist as he drew her inside the leaded, cedar door.

'Aren't you going to turn the lights on?' she whispered with a look of wild challenge.

'Enough, Claudia,' he moved her body right into his arms, his demeanour so masterful she felt frail and subjugated. 'Look up at me,' he demanded. 'It's childish to duck your head.'

I am not childish, she wanted to cry, but as she flung up her head, his fingers curled themselves in her hair dragging her head back while his mouth pressed down on hers.

It was so exquisite she thought her heart would break. She felt her body shudder and his arms enclosed her even more powerfully causing her to utter a little, gasping breath that he took into his mouth as his own.

'*Claudia!*' he muttered intensely and the effect on her was extraordinary.

Without conscious thought she pressed her body against his, clinging as if she would never let go. Her nostrils were filled with the wonderful male scent of him, while her delicate perfume hung like incense in the still darkness.

It was almost like extreme starvation for they were kissing with a keyed-up passion and hunger that went totally beyond anything they had experienced before. Nick wasn't holding back at all as he had on that other encounter but taking her with him so she lost all direction but his own.

The kissing went on for some time, until the pulses were beating thunderously in Claudia's veins. She tried to turn her heavy silken head begging him now as if the last of her innocence was slipping away. 'Nick . . . *please!*'

'Don't fight me.' His hands were at her narrow hips, moulding her fluttering body until she felt blasted with urgency.

'I can't *stand* this!' she lamented, but he held her and *held* her so she felt she would melt with the heat they were generating.

Wordlessly she hit him, helpless little blows, that did little to diminish the sexual agony. Her breasts were aching and he had not yet touched them. It was tantalising, tormenting as if being together were a punishment.

'I want you too much,' he said harshly, staring down at her as her upper body arched rigidly back. Her face revealed a terrible frustration, as dazzling as a pearl in the light that fell through the decorated glass panels. A nerve was clearly visible flickering in her neck and her mouth looked as soft and ripe as a fruit, faintly swollen and quite beautiful.

'Sweet God!' he said tightly.

Claudia's pain was beginning to turn to panic and though she couldn't recall it afterwards she was making little stricken sounds.

'Coffee, I think,' Nick suddenly announced abruptly and her heart bounded in a mixture of shock and disbelief. It didn't seem possible to turn from such extreme sensuality to mundane reality, but surely Nick had? Maybe his fascination was his total unpredictability.

The bright lights of the kitchen hurt her eyes and she put her hands to her cheeks, dazed. 'You're an extraordinary person, Nick.' A faint glistening of perspiration dewed her temples, her platinum hair was tumbled and her eyes looked like large, deep-green lakes.

'Thank you, darling,' he said suavely, very cool and self-contained. 'How would you like it— black or with cream?'

'Better make it a brandy.' She dropped into a chair, trying to reconcile such irreconcilable behaviour. He had gone out of his way to arouse her, succeeded cataclysmically, then pushed her into the kitchen. Surely a far from passionate place?

'Are you perfectly comfortable there?' he asked courteously.

'Don't worry about me, Nick.' Her lovely, low voice was very faintly slurred.

'Anything you'd like with it?'

'No.' She couldn't help it, she grimaced.

He bowed slightly, his lean handsome features vaguely wrenched for all his smoothness. 'I do have a backbone, Claudia,' he drawled, 'but it's very frail.'

'You're kidding!' She met his glittering, silver-grey eyes. 'I think you're very strong and madly practical.'

'I just thought it better to reserve our lovemaking for another occasion. Preferably the night we're married.'

It was a sharp, strange feeling to have him now mock her. 'Goodness, Nick,' she managed coolly, 'I never knew you were such a hopeless romantic.'

'To say nothing of *your* ability to stimulate desire.' He paused in his preparations to consider it. 'You know, darling, you look like an angel yet you're the most sexual woman I've ever known.'

She lifted a hand and thrust her heavy fall of hair back. 'Didn't your other women enjoy it?'

'I wasn't thinking of them so much as their effect on me.' Slowly he reached down some exquisite coffee cups that were used almost exclusively for best. 'Do you know I think I might have a toasted sandwich. I had a client who sat for hours this afternoon so I missed my lunch.'

'Gracious that will never do!' Claudia started up, spoiling it a little by swaying. 'I'm happy to make it for you.'

'Oh, don't worry,' Nick said briskly. 'You look so ravishing sitting there, all shocked eyes. I do wish you hadn't worn that dress. It's too easy to get out of.'

'Provided, of course, you were trying to get me out of it. Which you *aren't*.'

'I still *want* you,' he said, rather bitterly.

She wasn't quite sure what she was doing so she picked up one of the beautiful cobalt and gold coffee cups with its saucer, but her hands were so shaky, the saucer seemed to slide from her fingers.

'Woops.' Nick caught it very smartly and set it down on the table. 'Don't break them, darling. I'm too mean to buy more. Even if I could get them.'

'I'm sorry.' Bemusedly Claudia shook her head. 'And not at all safe.' In fact she found herself quite dizzy and as she lifted her eyes to

Nick he caught her behind the knees and folded her into his arms.

'Don't fret, baby. I feel the same.'

'I didn't know making love could be so ... violent.'

'It quite puts one off coffee, at any rate.'

'Where are you going, Nick?' She asked a little frantically as he carried her out of the room.

'It's one thing to leave you alone, darling, and quite another to see you giddy with frustration. I've been watching all the expressions that chase across your face. You want to sleep with me, don't you?'

'So long as you don't make love to me it should be all right.'

He gave a deep gurgle in his throat. 'All the thoughts I have of you when I'm in bed. I don't suppose you want to hear them?'

'No thank you.'

He began to move up the staircase and she cried out. There was a brittle humour in his face, but his eyes looked like a zealot's—ready to risk everything. 'If you've *planned* this, Nick!'

'Serves you right,' he said coolly. 'You're always telling me there's a demon in me.'

'And there *is*.'

'Settle down,' he said crisply. 'I'm only going to love you a little seeing there's nothing better I can do.'

When he lowered her to his bed she cried out remorsefully and rolled away on to her side. For a long time now she had imagined Nick's making love to her but the reality was rather more excessive than her wildest imaginings.

'At least I can get you out of that dress which,

incidentally makes you look like a rose.'

She sat up on her knees and as she did so she caught their reflections in the mirrored panel of the tall, antique wardrobe. The fuchsia silk of her full skirt did look like the petals of some extravagant rose. The sight of Nick made her heart lunge. He was seated sideways on the bed just behind her and he still had that bold, reckless light on him. She had never realised how striking the difference in their colouring. Her hair was white-gold. His very black, with no shade of brown. Her skin glimmered very palely, his had the sheen of dark, polished copper.

'You look impossibly erotic,' Nick said.

She thought she could bear it, but she couldn't. She tilted back her head and her eyes closed and that was the time he moved, drawing her back into his arms, his hands moving up over her small but exquisitely shaped breasts.

'Marry me, Claud,' he murmured. 'We desperately need each other.'

Her sense of unreality deepened. It was said so ardently she should have absolved him of all doubt. But there was Cristina. Or was she *mad*?

She let her head fall back against his shoulder, her mind drifting away from all disquietude.

His tongue rimmed the delicate whorls of her ear while he whispered she was beautiful to him. How could there be treachery in such ardour?

'How I wish you were mine.' His voice was a mere thread of sound. 'I could keep you through the night.' He covered her half-open mouth and she stayed his travelling hand and lifted it to her breast, understanding she was inviting a surge of male passion, more driving, more violent than a woman's could ever be.

'Claudia,' he murmured through the silk of her hair.

She could feel the faint shudder that racked his body, the emotional charge that was building up so rapidly it was like fire racing down the spine. Her dress had a bodice draped in a deep V and he slipped his hand inside the warm silk, cupping her tender, young breast enclosed in ivory lace. Claudia's breathing was more languorous now and the perfume she wore flowed from her heated skin in gentle wafts.

His fingers unclipped the lace bra and pushed it away, and her tremoring began.

'Marry me, please, Claudia,' he begged her. 'I'll cherish you. *Always.*'

Ecstasy overflowed her. No one but Nick could lift her to such a plane. His lovemaking was blissful. Perfect. More than that, it was causing her to offer herself to him as though it were her destiny.

Gradually he removed her dress: the warm, enveloping silk with little beneath. He turned away to drape it across his jacket and Claudia caught the flash of great passion on his face. His beautiful eyes gleamed and he looked infinitely in command of himself. And her. He looked at her as though she was a rare treasure. And *his* for the taking.

Some elusive rebellion swam in the depths of her surrender. By what right did men think they *owned* a woman? Yet in spite of her fragile mutiny she allowed him to discover many things about her he had never known before.

His mouth followed the smooth flow of her flesh and she sighed rapturously. It was a kind of primal submission, so infinitely soft yet fiery it became almost impossible to control her excitement.

'This is too dangerous, Claud.' Her urgent twistings were inciting him powerfully. 'If we don't stop now, I'll lose all control.'

She could have laughed she wanted it so enormously instead she pulled him ever closer, an astounding richness rife in her blood. 'You can, if you want, have *all* my secrets.'

He groaned and lifted his head. 'Do you want to save yourself, or not?'

'I think I like it too much here.'

'After all it's where you were meant to be.'

'*Really?*' Against that little flare of mutiny flashed out.

'Yes, really,' he mocked her. 'Man is still the hunter, my little Claudia, and I trapped you a long time ago.'

'I don't trap that easily.'

A faint smile touched his mouth. 'You make so much protest, Claudia. What about now when I'm holding your breasts like perfect fruit in my hands?'

Her voice had a beseeching, almost frantic tone. 'It's not possible to think clearly when you touch me.'

'Darling, are you ashamed to say it?'

She only turned her head and buried her face in the pillow. 'I think so.'

'Because Cristina has poisoned your mind?' Instantly the tenderness became grim disdain. 'Always we get back to that unhappy woman.'

'Maybe there's no escape.'

His hand closed hard under her chin as he

turned her to face him. 'And my word means *nothing*?' From disdain to developing anger.

She hesitated unhappily and it was a bad mistake. From the tenderness, protectiveness, that previously over-rode his passion, he seized her with near cruelty as though impelled to hear her cry of fright.

He lifted her without effort . . . she lay on top then beneath him, his hands moving over her body so she was in an agony of furious pleasure. Her strength was as nothing against his, but even as he shocked her, she knew herself thrilled to be mastered.

When the longing became unbearable little inarticulate moans were dragged out of her and only then did he leave her, lifting his lean body away as if in contempt.

'Hell, isn't it?' he stood over her, his dark face saturnine.

She still lay across the bed in a half tortured position, pierced by the glacial glitter of his eyes.

'What's the matter, Claudia?' he taunted her. 'Have I spoiled something for you? You're spoiling everything for me.'

Her heavy white-gold hair flew around her face as she raised herself up. 'So have your ring back,' she cried, extending her left hand while the emerald glowed like green fire against her white skin. 'Haven't I always known you're a dozen men rolled into one. You're too complicated Nick.'

'Sure.' His fine, white teeth were set on edge. 'And I feel at times you're quite stupid.'

'I *am*!' She clutched wildly for a sheet.

'And how!' Despite his anger his eyes were ravished by the gleaming image she presented.

He stood still for another minute staring at her then he moved back and plucked her dress off a chair. 'The next time, my little Claudia, you want me to make love to you, you're going to have to *beg* for it.'

'Don't worry, I haven't the slightest doubt I will!'

And then he laughed. Genuine amusement this time. 'You don't kid yourself do you, sweetheart?'

'What the hell!' Like a half wild creature she got into her clothes. 'You must be used to my odd behaviour. I can't seem to take a positive stand about anything with you. I must be mad or mesmerised or both. I offer you everything you want . . .'

'*Except* trust,' he interrupted metallically.

'*Please*, Nick!' she rose up on the bed, joining her hands together as though in fervent prayer. 'Don't you think I want to. Do you really think I like torturing myself?'

'Yes,' he said bluntly. 'Yes, I do.' The obvious signs of strain were on him. 'I've had nothing but accusations and recriminations for months. More than enough to endure. I don't think you care about me as much as you think you do. To be dismissed so abruptly with this talk of a fallen idol! If it didn't sound so conceited, I'd tell you a lot of fool women have fallen in love with me. Women I didn't *ask* to. Maybe it's natural for women to want men that won't take them seriously. The thing is, I *love you*, Claud. I even want to marry you and that's a very big thing. For one, you're so beautiful it's going to be difficult keeping you to myself.'

It was so utterly unexpected she jerked back her head. 'But, Nick, that's *crazy*! I would never look at anyone at all.'

'How do you know? You're just a baby. Wait until you're thirty and fully aware of your power. Wait until another man falls under your spell. Tells you he loves you.'

She was so astonished she slipped off the bed and came to him. 'Is this the supremely self-confident Nick Grey talking?' she asked incredulously.

'Maybe I am. In a way.' He stood with his arms linked around her. 'But I'm helpless with you.'

'I don't believe it.' Her green eyes searched his face.

'Incredible! A beautiful woman without ego. Anyway, it's *true*.'

It was totally different from anything she had thought to hear him say. She leant against him and closed her eyes. 'Do you swear to love only me?'

'Try me.' His tone was curt to the point of hardness.

'You could hurt me terribly. Worse, destroy me.' She tilted back her head.

'We could destroy one another.' His silver eyes were deadly serious.

'I'll be faithful to you, Nick. I promise.' Impulsively she reached up and kissed his chin, but he dropped a hard, sober kiss on her mouth. 'I'm counting on that. I'd like you to remain *alive*.'

She couldn't believe the odd ruthlessness of his expression. She put her arms around him, hugging him, holding her head against his breast. 'Do you really, under it all, despise women?'

'They make excellent adultresses,' he said coolly.

She was alarmed. '*Nick!* It never occurred to me for one minute to think you were a hater of women.'

'Nor did it occur to you to believe I love *you* totally. That's the total passion I'm *capable* of, Claudia.'

'Yes, Nick.'

'I mean what I say.'

She could feel the tension in him, making his lean body rock hard. 'I'll marry you, Nick, whenever you want.'

'Loving me would be infinitely better,' he told her with faint bitterness. 'You're very valuable to me for your beauty, but that's only a part of it. I want your heart and your mind. I don't want to see you fall so easily into traps. Respect between a man and woman is very important. It can't be otherwise for us.'

'Of course, Nick,' Tears stood in her eyes. 'I see it now. I believe you.'

'Almost.' He brushed the hair away from her face. 'Would you let me take you now to prove it?'

'Yes.' Her gaze was steady.

'And I love you too much to order it,' he stared into her eyes. 'When you come to me, Claudia, it will be of your own free will.'

CHAPTER SEVEN

THE days continued with Cristina still incredibly sour and bitchy.

'If it weren't for Claudia,' Fergy confided wearily, 'I'd walk out. I've never seen a woman so restless and irritable.'

'Maybe it's because she's put on weight?' Lady McKinlay suggested. The three of them were at work in the McKinlay sunroom writing out invitations for one of Lady McKinlay's charity functions. 'Grant really should have insisted on a break together instead of which he's left it.'

'He's very busy, Nanna,' Claudia said, feeling as terrible as any of them.

'Maybe, but from what little I've seen of Cristina, she appears to be heading for some sort of breakdown. These busy, self-confident career women can be classic cases.'

'It's not even a case of fluctuating moods,' Fergy said aggrievedly. 'She's sharp and over-aggressive all the time.'

'The trouble could be physical,' Lady McKinlay offered worriedly. 'It's unusual for Cristina surely? Has she had a check up?'

Fergy shrugged as if to say she couldn't care less, but Claudia sighed. 'I think she's in need of a complete change. Daddy hates all the disorderliness in the house.'

'Ah, yes,' Lady McKinlay chose to say no more. She knew her son-in-law's good qualities just as she knew he resented any complications whatever in the home. Claudia herself had never told her father anything else than what he wanted to hear. As a daughter she had been remarkably trouble free and it didn't just happen. Even as a child Claudia had recognised what her father had required of her so she had worked hard at presenting herself in his image. No tantrums for Claudia. No escapades. No troublesome behaviour so life could run smoothly. Nevertheless Claudia had plenty of character and spirit under that lovely, cool exterior. Lady McKinlay stopped what she was doing and on the spur of the moment leant over and kissed Claudia's cheek.

'What's *that* for?' Claudia smiled.

'I love you,' Lady McKinlay said, straightening up. 'Now, where did I put those envelopes?'

Shortly before mid-day a telephone call came for Claudia. 'It's your father,' Fergy came back into the sunroom to tell her. 'He sounds upset.'

'Oh Heavens!' Claudia whispered.

'Answer it, darling,' Lady McKinlay said practically. 'Grant's upsets are on a slightly different scale.'

Grant Ingram came to the point immediately. 'Cristina has been taken to hospital,' he told Claudia bleakly. 'It appears she collapsed at a client's home and they got such a fright they ordered an ambulance.'

Lady McKinlay and Fergy looked at her expectantly as she walked back into the sunroom. 'Cristina is in hospital,' she announced.

'Dear me!' Lady McKinlay went a little limp. 'Whatever has happened?'

'We don't really know. Daddy is leaving for the hospital now. It seems she collapsed at a client's house. They called for an ambulance and it took her to the P.A.'

'Poor girl!'

'Mind you, she doesn't eat enough,' Fergy said. 'For all she's put on weight lately as you said.'

'Surely she couldn't be having a baby?' Lady McKinlay marvelled and Claudia went white with shock. 'I say, dear,' Lady McKinlay exclaimed as the older women jumped to their feet. 'Here, hold her head down, Fergy.'

'Claudy, darling!' Fergy's hands shook pathetically even as she rushed to obey.

'I'm all right,' Claudia's voice sounded weak and far away. She was fighting to pull back from a faint.

'Fergy go and get Ross,' Lady McKinlay ordered, holding Claudia's forehead. 'He's in his study.'

By the time her grandfather arrived, Claudia was out of it. 'What happened, darling,' he asked calmly, holding her wrist.

'I don't know. I just started to black out,' she laughed shakily.

'You've never done such a thing before,' he said watching her very closely.

'She's just had a shock,' Lady McKinlay explained. 'Cristina has been taken to the hospital.'

'Good God!' Sir Ross stared up at his wife. 'Was that the phone call?'

'Yes. She collapsed on the job. Grant rang.'

'I just walked out of the study for a moment,'

Sir Ross said regretfully. 'I could have taken that call. What hospital?'

'The P.A.'

'I'll go over.'

'*Would* you Granddad?' Claudia's colour was returning.

'Was *that* it, darling?' Sir Ross asked her.

She glanced away from his all-seeing eyes. 'The news upset me.'

'Perhaps.' Sir Ross turned his handsome head. 'Tea, Fergy, if you wouldn't mind. Three teaspoons of sugar.'

'Grandad, I couldn't *drink* it.'

'Two and a half then.' Calmly, deliberately, Sir Ross examined his granddaughter's face. 'How long is it since you've had a check up?'

'I'm never sick, Grandad, you know that?'

'True. Nevertheless a check up won't hurt. I'll call Anthony later today and let you know. Of course you're upset about Cristina. But a *faint*?'

'I *didn't* faint.'

'Darned nearly,' Lady McKinlay put her arm around her granddaughter. 'Was it what I said, about the baby?'

'*What* baby?' Sir Ross threw his arm out in surprise.

'Sweetheart, don't panic,' Lady McKinlay said. 'Cristina has been very much out of sorts lately and she's put on weight. I just put two and two together.'

'Then I don't care to bet you're wrong,' Sir Ross concluded from long experience. 'Does it seem likely to you, Claudia?'

'I don't know.' Claudia could have fallen to the floor and sobbed. A baby? *Whose* baby? She hated herself for thinking as she did but there was the most terrible doubt in her heart.

'Claudia, darling, there's something more to this than you're saying,' Sir Ross took her hands. 'If the news were true and we're only jumping to conclusions, why would it upset you?'

Lady McKinlay's smile was full of sadness. 'What *is* it, dearest?'

'It *can't* be,' Claudia managed. 'Why would Cristina be so secretive?'

'Suppose we take one thing at a time,' Sir Ross suggested. 'Would you like to come to the hospital with me? It would set your mind at rest.'

'But Cristina has never wanted a baby!' Claudia looked back at her grandfather appealingly.

'That's what they all say,' Lady McKinlay murmured dryly. 'Cristina would be a lot happier with a child in her life. And your father would look on it as miraculous.'

'We would be happy too if she were pregnant,' Sir Ross said, watching his granddaughter's eyes. '*Wouldn't* we, darling?'

'Of course.' Claudia's whole body seemed tied in knots.

'Yes, well . . .' Lady McKinlay said a shade inadequately, 'At this moment we know nothing for sure.' She looked towards the doorway and her face changed to relief. 'Ah, here's Fergy with the tea.'

'Better now?' Fergy sought the opinion from Sir Ross.

'Yes, she's coming around slowly.' He patted his granddaughter's hand. 'We'll sit quietly for an hour then we'll go to the hospital. I'll give Victor Thornton a ring.'

When they arrived at the hospital Matron herself showed them to Cristina's bedside. She had been put into a ward and Sir Ross had already been apprised of her condition. Cristina was indeed pregnant: some eight weeks along the way.

Cristina lay quiet, one long hand outside the sheet across her breast. Grant Ingram was seated by her side, his expression an odd mixture of intense gratification and a faint unease.

'Cristina, my dear!' Sir Ross made Cristina look up with a tearful smile.

'Oh, Sir Ross!' Now the tears came easily.

'There, there, my dear. This is wonderful news.' He bent his head and kissed her on the cheek. 'A baby is the most wonderful gift of all. I've spoken to Dr Thornton and apart from overdoing it a little, you're in excellent health.'

'None of this mad rushing around again!' Grant Ingram, now that his father-in-law was on the scene began to laugh. No matter what, Ross McKinlay had this marvellously calming presence. Before he had arrived Cristina had scarcely spoken.

'How are you, Cristina?' Claudia touched her stepmother's hand.

'So-so,' Cristina turned to her a white, freckled face. 'It was nice of you to come.'

'I could beat her for not saying anything to me,' Grant Ingram enthused. 'This is just the most wonderful news. I can't take it in.'

'Cristina doesn't look happy to be an expectant mother,' Claudia said to her grandfather on the way home.

'She's a little scared at the moment, darling,' Sir Ross replied easily. 'Some women become

quite shocked when they receive the news.
Marriage may be a big commitment but a child
is the biggest commitment of all. It will make a
big difference to Cristina and your father is
halfway over the moon. He'd be all the way
over I'm sure only Cristina is having her little
difficulties adjusting. The thirties is a little late
to come to motherhood. I think she feels a little
awkward. She was so set in her career and she's
feeling upset about the physical changes in her
body. It's a state a lot of women go through.
Not everyone is ecstatic from the beginning.
She's a tall woman. She should carry her baby
well. If anything, I'm more concerned about
you. You're not quite yourself these days, are
you?'

'It takes a little adjusting being an engaged
girl,' she said wryly.

'Yet you love Nick deeply.'

'I do.' And that was the crazy, screaming truth
of it.

'And he loves you.'

'Do you *really* think so, Grandad?'

'Ah, how frail we human creatures are!' Sir
Ross mused reflectively. 'How intensely unsure
in our relationships. I suppose, my darling,
you've had a fantasy romance with Nick for as
long as you've known him. Thirteen, fourteen is a
very particular stage in a young girl's develop-
ment. For the very first time she feels the
stirrings of sexual love. I think you fell in love
with Nick right off though it was subdued from a
conscious level. Fortunately you fell in love with
the right man. Nick was equally attracted to you.
He was incredibly fond of you as you must

remember then as time went on there was this enormous change. The fact is, Claudia, Nick has acted supremely well in your case. He's drawn back from any closer relationship for a number of factors. You were too young; too inexperienced; you hadn't completed your education; you had to experience the admiration and attention of other young men. He gave you a chance to form other relationships. To a large extent to grow up. And why? Because he loves you. Really loves you. He cherished and protected you as a child and young girl, but being a man of strong passions, I guess his capacity for waiting is exhausted. I'd say it would be apparent to a blind man he's madly in love with you.'

'You haven't considered he's a marvellous actor?'

'*Claudia!*' Sir Ross was so shocked he slowed the car and brought it to a halt. 'Whatever are you saying?' He switched off the ignition and turned to her.

'I think in some deep way Nick feels safe with me. We've known one another for so long and I'm a very *quiet* person, aren't I, Grandad?'

'You mean you have a lovely, gentle composure, don't you? Quiet is not at all the right word.'

'All right then, I'm not *vibrant*.'

'What *are* we talking about, Claudia?' Sir Ross asked tersely. 'There's something very much on your mind and I think you'd better tell me.'

She shook her head. How could she tell her grandfather *that*? How could she upset him? He thought the world of Nick. The whole thing was *horrible*.

'Has it something to do with Cristina?' Sir

Ross asked sternly. 'I've lived a long time, my darling. I've got eyes.'

'I just feel a little frightened at the moment, Grandad. Very unsure of myself. Which way to go.'

'Have you ever considered you might *lose* Nick, if you're not more positive, more trusting in your outlook?'

'*Grandad!*' Claudia's voice was a funny, little croak.

Sir Ross nodded slowly. 'I think we in the family have been all aware of Cristina's—how shall we put it—crush on Nick?'

Claudia looked stunned. 'You've never said *one* word to me. Neither you nor Nanna.'

'What could we say? We just prayed in time it would go away. Nick is an extremely handsome man. As well as that he's so clever and he has great charm of manner. He has so much going for him it's no wonder most women let out whoops of joy. His mother was like that, you know. She was the most *fascinating* woman. You have no idea. When *she* came into a room, other women used to fade. Not just her beauty alone. She was almost unbearably attractive. I'm afraid we all knew poor old Grey would never hold her. It's the greatest mystery how she ever married him in the first place, but she did, just like that! And tragically as it happened. A terrible tragedy all round.'

Claudia nodded emphatically. 'It affected Nick deeply.'

'Yes, he was left very much alone. Lang Somerville was a splendid fellow but way past the age for rearing a young boy. In effect, you know, *we* have been Nick's family. We're all very attached to him as he is to us. Your father has looked on him as a son. He's done everything to advance Nick's career.'

'So Nick might be repaying him in marrying me?'

'Oh rubbish!' Sir Ross said shortly. 'Really, Claudia, you're far too perceptive to make such an absurd statement. Nick's been in emotional turmoil about you for years. Many's the time I felt sorry for him.'

'Sorry for him with all his lady friends?' Claudia cried scornfully.

'What did you expect him to do?' Sir Ross asked blandly. 'He couldn't have you. The fact is he brightened a few lives. I can't think of one woman friend who still doesn't speak to him on the telephone. I don't think Nick has misled anybody.'

'Cristina claims Nick has had an affair with her,' Claudia suddenly burst out. It didn't make sense. She had been determined not to say it yet the words had gushed from her.

'To *hell* with Cristina!' Uncharacteristically Sir Ross swore. 'The woman's a liar.' He was so outraged the blood had come to his cheeks.

'I shouldn't have told you,' Claudia said. 'I never meant to. It just sprang out.'

'Of course you should have told me,' Sir Ross said with utter conviction. 'Fancy keeping a thing like this to yourself, Claudia, when you have your grandmother and me to talk to. This whole thing is preposterous. You said yourself Cristina has been erratic in her behaviour. There's no telling what a female will say and do at different stages of her life.'

'*I'm* a female, Granddad.'

'Women are given a lot to fantasising,' Sir Ross amended. 'Link it to hormonal changes if you like. Cristina has told you this nonsense, how *dare* she, when the balance of her mind has been disturbed. It's far too early for the menopause. It must be some underlying psychological disorder. Really, it's quite extraordinary.'

'Nick denies it.' Claudia spoke in a subdued whisper.

'Poor old Nick!' Sir Ross cried. 'Fancy associating *Nick* with such lunacy. Nick with your *father's wife*? What is the world coming to, I ask you!'

'Please don't be upset, Grandad,' Claudia begged.

'My dear child,' he turned to her, 'you seem to have turned it to private grief.'

'It's been dreadful, Grandad.' The tears stood in her eyes.

'My darling girl.' Sadly Sir Ross shook his head. 'It must be because you're so young, so fine and innocent in your mind, Cristina has been allowed to feed you such a tale. Surely you can see that Nick loves you?'

'He *wants* me, Grandad,' Claudia said baldly.

'Of course he wants you!' Sir Ross shrugged impatiently. 'Dear Heaven, Claudia, a man desperately wants the woman he loves. Be grateful for it. Your grandmother has such marvellous intuition yet she hasn't suspected all this nonsense.'

'I saw them together.'

'*What?*' Sir Ross's green eyes blackened.

'At least, Nick was at the house one afternoon

when everyone was out. I arrived home un-expectedly to see Cristina flying down the gallery after him in a negligee.'

'I don't care if she was flying down the gallery after him stark naked,' Sir Ross shouted. 'Nothing in this world can persuade me Nick has acted in any way dishonourably with your father's wife.'

'God forgive me for not sharing your trust,' Claudia now wept.

'This is dreadful, *dreadful*!' Sir Ross said. 'Surely Grant hasn't an inkling of all this?'

'Daddy doesn't know.'

'Then it's about time he did.'

'Oh, *no*, Grandad. I would rather die than upset him.'

'Wouldn't you just,' Sir Ross said grimly. 'It's strange how some people go through life being protected by everyone else. Everything, every-thing, has to be done for Grant's pleasure and comfort. He had a rare and lovely wife . . . he has a rare and lovely daughter . . .'

'*Please*, Grandad.' Claudia could see how upset her grandfather was becoming. 'Forgive me for starting all this. I love you so much. Forgive me.'

'Poor old *Nick*!' Sir Ross spluttered again. 'Do you mean to tell me, my girl, that you've told him you ever believed in this rubbish?'

'Because Cristina told me many times. I find it impossible to believe she could tell such an appalling lie.'

'And equally impossible Nick, *our* Nick, *your* Nick, could come down to such a sordid arrangement.'

'However hard I try there has always been this element of doubt,' Claudia confessed bleakly.

'Yet you became engaged? How *could* you, believing such a thing?'

'It was a frightful mix-up,' Claudia inadequately explained.

'It's good of you to tell me now,' Sir Ross said extremely dryly. 'So when you heard Cristina might be pregnant, you thought of the most unnatural thing possible?'

'Yes.' Claudia hung her head.

'Dear God!' Sir Ross struck the steering wheel. 'You do well to hang your head in shame.'

Claudia cried.

'What a messy business!' Sir Ross handed her his clean handkerchief.

'I have to cry sometimes.'

'I mean this ... *lunacy*!' Sir Ross was back to shouting and he had a fine, resonant voice. 'I won't speak to Nick. I don't have to.'

'I've spoken to him about it for months.'

'Then it's a test of his love you're still together.'

'If you had a crush on somebody,' Claudia said huskily, 'could you possibly behave in such a destructive way?'

'I shall have to spend some time with one of my psychiatrist friends,' Sir Ross replied wryly. 'I'm not sorry for your stepmother. I'm too angry. I always thought her a quite sensible woman. Of course the marriage was pretty much convenience. An adult sort of thing. Which is not to say they both didn't *care* about each other. Superficially I was sure they were well matched. Your father suffered as much as he was able when Victoria died. I think he just stashed away love on that deep level. The pain was too much.

Certainly he was very slow to remarry but he and Cristina developed a mature relationship. They were reasonably happy, surely? They certainly gave that impression.'

'They *were* happy,' Claudia said hastily. 'Nick was overseas for a lot of that first year, don't you remember?'

'Hah!' Sir Ross burst out with a most terrible contempt. 'Don't try to tell me it was on from then?'

'I know he *unsettled* her,' Claudia said.

'So? He's very attractive. I told you about his mother. Some people are really special. They have a kind of sexual radiance, I suppose. Do you know a lot of my patients used to fall in love with *me*. Or so they tell me. Little harmless fantasies, you know. Like reading a book or seeing a film with your favourite movie star. I used to be madly in love with Vivien Leigh at one time. Most people go in for harmless daydreams at different times.'

'Only this is something awful.'

'A canker in the brain. No, Claudia, I simply don't believe it. Your stepmother may have tried to compromise Nick in some way, but you can be absolutely certain of one thing; it's not *his* child she's having. You'd have done better to call her bluff than swallow her poison cold. And you can't, absolutely *can't*, allow Nick to see your terrible doubts. You'll lose him if you keep it up. He has his pride. In fact he's fiercely proud and in many ways he's had a hard life. We all have our capacity for tolerance. You say you've spoken to Nick about this for months, which when I think about it, is *shocking*. How can you say you *love*, Nick, when you're prepared to take Cristina's word against his?'

'I keep thinking that myself, Grandad. Maybe I'm not worthy to love him. Maybe I have no sense at all. It just seemed to me beyond reason that Cristina should lie.'

'Partly that and you just don't appreciate your position in his life. You *are* young. Cristina is much older and far more experienced. To put the matter simply, she has used this to inflict cruelty and hurt. I find it difficult to believe it of her but it must be true. Certainly Nick was never attracted to her. One can spot these things. Actually, Claudia, my darling, nothing *fits*. I would say Cristina's frustrated yearning turned rotten. Or it has up to date. Why she picked on Nick is understandable. He's very much around and he's highly desirable. Why she picked on you is another thing again. Perhaps she feels her loss of youth greatly. Perhaps she feels she missed out somehow along the line. Her first marriage so far as I can make out was a disaster and her second was largely to create a lifestyle. Not good enough, you know, for marriage. Maybe the baby will resolve all these difficulties. It's extremely inappropriate for an expectant mother to be out of love with her husband.' Sir Ross turned to his granddaughter and laid his hand along her cheek. 'Does this make any sense to you, darling?'

'It must, Grandad. You're the wisest person in the world.'

Cristina was discharged from hospital the following morning. It was a Saturday and Grant Ingram had been downstairs for hours. Finally he

climbed the stairs to his daughter's room. Claudia
had slept badly, accepting her grandfather's
censure and in no mood to feel ecstatic about the
wonderful news.

'Claudia, dear, may I come in?'

Claudia had taken a shower and washed her
hair, now she was resting in the golden sunlight
that streamed through her three, tall windows.

'Good morning, Daddy.' She stood up to greet
him as he advanced into the room.

'Good morning, darling. Glorious morning it is
too!' As usual he was very smartly dressed, but
there was an extra spring in his step and he put
his arm around his daughter and fondly kissed
her. 'I wanted to have breakfast with you.'

'Oh I'm sorry, I slept in.'

'You do look a little heavy eyed.' He looked
down into her creamy face. 'You're pleased about
this wonderful news, aren't you, darling?'

'Of course I am, Daddy. I'm *thrilled* for you.'

'I knew you would be. You're such a lovely
person. Sometimes I get a terrible shock. I look
at you sometimes and it's Vicki. My beautiful
Victoria. I never dwell on it because for a long
time now I've had part of my heart in cold
storage. Maybe it even died. Losing your mother
was the most terrifying thing that ever happened
to me. I knew I couldn't face anything like that
again.'

'No, it must have been terrible,' Claudia
quietly said. Didn't her father ever realise she too
lost her mother. No one should be without a
mother.

'I never thought to marry again and I was
happy enough in my ivory tower. I had *you*. I had

your grandparents. They've always been marvellous support. Finally Cristina came along. Our friendship had a different quality. I like a woman to have a certain amount of self sufficiency and I'd had all I ever needed of heart-stopping love. Cristina seemed a woman to share the rest of my life with. She told me she didn't want children and I accepted that. I had you. Now everything has changed. I thought Cristina had been unusually moody but now we know the cause of it. She told me she was careless with her birth control pills yet in a sense this has really shocked her. She can't believe she's pregnant. Can you beat that?'

'Not really, Daddy.' She forgot her pills. She's of child-bearing age. Whenever had she answered like that?

'You know this will make no difference to you and me?' Grant Ingram said reassuringly. 'You look rather desperately poignant,' he added softly.

'I will *adore* to have a little brother,' Claudia said. Better not make it a *sister*, Cristina, she thought.

'Darling girl!' Grant Ingram pressed her to his side. 'I can't wait to tell Nick.'

'We're driving down the coast this afternoon.'

'Yes, I know. What say we *all* go and make it a celebration dinner?'

'I don't think Cristina will be feeling up to it.'

'Possibly not.' Grant Ingram's fine eyes were soft. 'We'll have it at some other time. What a mercy she's missed out on morning sickness! I remember your mother felt terrible in her early days.'

They talked for a few more minutes and Grant Ingram said goodbye. For weeks he had found the situation with his wife quite stressful now all that had changed. There was joy in his life again. Claudia was the image of her mother but his son would have *his* looks, *his* eyes. Just when he thought his life was almost over, he had entered on a new, wonderful phase.

'Your Dad's happy!' Fergy commented laconically.

'Oh, Fergy, no breakfast for me.'

'Don't be silly.' Fergy pulled out a chair and beckoned Claudia into it. 'You are *my* baby. Your father will never have another child like you.'

'He doesn't *want* one like me, Fergy,' Claudia sat down with a soft sigh. 'I pray Cristina's baby will be a boy.'

'Don't fret,' Fergy said astonishingly, 'it will be. So long as it isn't a little monster like its mother.'

'Well,' Claudia said, 'he will be my little brother. I know I'll love him ... her ... whatever.'

'You might be able to mind him while his mother goes out to work.'

'This baby might change everything, Fergy,' Claudia said hopefully and sipped at her orange juice.

'The only baby I'm going to get dotty about from now on is *yours*.'

'You might have a long wait.'

'I don't think so,' Fergy gurgled. 'Maybe a year of being together, then the year after that. Has Nick heard the news?'

'No.'

'I'd just like to see his face.'

'So would I.' Very quietly Claudia set down her spoon, but Fergy was busy serving up scrambled eggs. 'We all thought your stepmother preferred a career to having babies.'

'Lots of women start off like that only to find they'd prefer the latter. Family is everything, isn't it? To see your children growing.'

'Your mother would be very proud of you,' Fergy said emotionally. 'And how she would give her blessing to your marriage with Nick. He's everything we want for you, and don't you worry, *he'll* be wanting a pretty little *girl*. *You* were very popular as I recall. Though little sister wasn't exactly what Nick had in mind. Actually I think he deserves a decoration. He's done everything in his power not to imperil your soul.'

Claudia shook her head as though all this was very new to her. 'Now that Cristina is pregnant, I think I'll get a place of my own.'

'You mean you're leaving?' Fergy asked flatly.

'Things have changed, Fergy,' Claudia said.

'Yes, the old days have simply vanished.' Fergy inched a cup of tea closer to Claudia's hand. 'I can't stay here without you, love. You ought to know that. I stayed for you and when you go I go too.'

Claudia nodded, then she put her head in her hands. 'I think Daddy will take it all right.'

'*I* don't,' Fergy said. 'Can't you stick it out until you and Nick get married? What are you waiting for anyway? The way Nick looks at you I wonder he hasn't made you set the date. Your Grandma now has spoken to me about the whole thing. She knows I've never liked Cristina much.

She wants me to come to her. She's out so much of the time and Sir Ross is becoming involved in so many things these days, I would be a big help to them.'

'And what about *me*?' Claudia blinked. 'You've been everything to me while I've been growing up.'

'Well, that's easy,' Fergy smiled and covered Claudia's hand with her own. 'I'll be Nanny when the first baby arrives.'

Cristina came home looking stooped and frail. Moreover, she was sobbing quietly into her husband's shoulder.

'How's that for freakish behaviour?' Fergy said.

Later they were informed she had taken to her bed.

'You don't suppose she's going to turn into an invalid?' Fergy asked.

'It must be a big shock finding out you're going to be a mother,' Claudia said charitably but without a great deal of enthusiasm. Cristina had behaved abominably in so many ways, there was no feeling sympathetic towards her. She had been especially overbearing with Fergy so it was small wonder Fergy had begun making plans to move out.

Claudia seized a quiet moment with her father to broach her own intentions. Nick wasn't due for an hour and things really couldn't go on as they were.

'How is Cristina now?'

'Much better.' Grant Ingram settled back in his armchair comfortably. 'Do you know I quite like her with her hair loose and not so much make-up.'

'So do I.' That morning at least Cristina had fallen down on the job, but she *had* looked softer and younger. 'May I speak to you about something, Daddy?' Claudia, in her bright beach clothes sank into the chair opposite her father.

'Of course, darling.' He had picked up the morning paper, now he set it down, his underlying pleasure and excitement keeping his mood buoyant.

'Don't you think it's time I had a place of my own?'

At her words her father's expression changed. 'My dear girl, what on earth for? I firmly believe a daughter should be married from her own home. Good God, isn't the house *big* enough?'

'The fact is Cristina may like to feel the mistress of her own home. Things are different now, Daddy, or will Cristina still be rushing out to work?'

'I certainly don't want her to,' Grant Ingram maintained. 'Actually though she's quite healthy she has been told she can't go through her days at the same hectic pace. How do you think she collapsed in the first place?'

'Exactly.' Claudia pressed her case. 'Cristina and I get on well,' (how odd a statement), 'but I can't be forever in her hair. I think she needs the house to herself but she's too tactful to say so.'

'Be that as it may,' Grant Ingram said flatly. 'I need you both. In any case you and Nick will be getting married. You can move out then. Of course I realise you're trying to see Cristina's side of it but I think you'll discover she'll reach out to you now. She seems so *needy* since she found out. You saw her crying and clinging to me. When did Cristina ever *cling*? No, there's been a big change in her. When she settles I know she's going to be as ecstatic as I am. This baby is going to bring something deep to our marriage. Something that wasn't there before. It will be a total marriage as it ought to be. It will make Cristina a *real* woman. Already she's softer and more womanly. No, Claudia, I want you to stay. You're my daughter and that's the way it should be and furthermore I take the view you and Cristina will grow closer together. She's a little distraught at the moment and she's going to need help and support. Why don't you pop upstairs now and say hello?'

'Later, Daddy,' Claudia said. 'She may be resting.'

When Nick's car came up the drive Grant Ingram jumped to his feet, throwing a smiling look back over his shoulder. 'I wonder what Nick will make of the news?'

Claudia just stood there, wide eyed. Her grandfather's advice was still ringing in her ears, but like some all powerful nightmare that one couldn't break out of, she was tensed for some thrust that might kill her.

Her father opened the front door and Claudia heard Nick's voice. 'Good morning, Grant. You're looking extraordinarily fit and well.'

'I am. Come in, Nick. Come in. We have some astonishing news for you.'

'Thank God it's good. It is good isn't it?' Nick looked towards Claudia and held out his hand.

She went to him and he slipped an arm around her and kissed her cheek.

'Do you care to tell Nick, darling?' Grant Ingram beamed.

'No, it's your news, Daddy.'

'Oh?' Nick glanced down at her and his expression seemed to harden. He had seen in her face what others did not. The marshalling of all her courage in the face of severe shock.

'Please, let's all sit down for a moment.' With bright impatience Grant Ingram led them into the living room. 'The fact is, Nick, my boy, my wife is expecting a baby.'

For a few seconds it seemed to have no effect on Nick whatever. He continued to look at Claudia sitting so rigidly beside him, then he turned his head and addressed his senior partner.

'This is wonderful news, Grant.'

'*Wonderful!*'

Nick stood up, walked to the older man, clapped him on the shoulder, then shook his hand. 'I'm very happy for you, Grant.'

'I knew you would be.' Grant Ingram's face was almost brilliant with light. 'It's only early days yet. I'd open a bottle of champagne only you're driving to the coast.'

'We'll have it yet.' The two men continued to clasp hands.

While Claudia remained silent Grant Ingram went on to outline the events of the day before. 'Claudia was so shocked she almost *fainted*!' Grant Ingram laughed. 'Her grandfather was so concerned he has organised a check-up for her Monday morning.'

'*Has* he?' Nick looked at Claudia with

unsmiling eyes. With his dark summer tan his
eyes were pure silver and what she saw in them
made her shiver.

Finally they were able to walk to the car
together. After Grant Ingram's exuberance they
had nothing to say to each other. Indeed they
covered some considerable distance before
Claudia spoke the first words.

'So Daddy will have his son.' Her soft voice
trembled a little.

'You're quite *certain* of that?' He looked very
ruthless and strong.

'Well, I'll keep praying.'

'What exactly *for*, my dearest?'

'You know how Daddy has longed for a son.
He would be very disappointed if another
daughter were born.'

'I'm glad not all of us are so afflicted,' Nick
returned curtly. 'There are plenty of men like *me*
who would adore to have a girl-child.'

'I know that, Nick,' she said placatingly.
'We're all so different and I'm grateful for it.'

'What *else* are you grateful for?'

'I don't think you should get angry in a car like
this,' she said carefully. 'We seem to be moving a
lot faster than everyone else.' Indeed they were
flying up the right lane.

Nick's eyes dropped to the speedometer he had
forgotten. 'So we are. I wonder if there's a
motorcycle cop mad to take me on.'

'It could prove expensive.'

'We need an autobahn for this car.'

'Then you'll have to take it abroad.'

For the rest of the trip they talked, by common
consent, about architecture, though Claudia's

mind constantly leapt ahead to the formidable confrontation that had to come. She could never learn to be an actress. Never learn to disguise her deepest thoughts with a practised smile.

On that summer's day the ocean was an incredible, glittering turquoise and Nick drove on until he found a spot where they had a stretch of golden beach to themselves. Near the edge the water was as clear as crystal but as it grew deeper it shaded into its deep and brilliant blue. Such glorious beaches ran almost continuously down the east coast of Australia, thousands of miles of big and beautiful surf.

'Is it your intention to swim?' Nick asked with exaggerated politeness.

'Of course it's my intention to swim.' She was dismayed by his coldness, though she tried to cling to some semblance of normal pleasantness. 'I've even bought a new swimsuit.'

'Terrific.' Nick set them up on the dazzling sand; umbrella, yellow with a deep white fringe, towels, her beach bag, two small folding beach chairs, the esky Fergy had packed for them. 'I can't find fault with your *body*.'

She ignored him and pulled her short, cotton smock over her head, feeling the rush of balmy, salt air over her newly exposed skin. She was wearing a red bikini with a black spot and there wasn't one inch of her that was in need of reformation. In fact she looked a dream, but Nick offered no remark. He stripped to navy briefs his body very evenly darkly tanned, greyhound lean and athletic, then he loped away from her to the water.

The important thing, Claudia decided, was to

act as though she had never inflicted on him a moment's doubt but all the time she had the dreadful feeling he had finally judged her and found her badly wanting. For that matter, she deserved it. The recognition was like light breaking through darkness. She deserved total rejection. It was as simple as that. As simple as her grandfather had found it to be. Her grandfather was genuinely wise whereas she was devastatingly inexperienced at making judgments.

Nevertheless the water was so glorious it seemed to go a way towards transforming Nick's mood. He sported like a dolphin, moving through the water with a speed and power she could never hope to match, though she swam particularly well.

After twenty minutes she went in to sunbathe, but Nick stayed out. Evidently he was far happier in the water than he was with her. Her grandfather had warned her Nick might cut her out of his life and it was obvious this morning she had made, yet again, a dreadful mistake. Why had she failed him. *Why?* Was she so astonished that he had said he loved her? Was she genuinely afraid of his enormous power over her?

'That was *glorious*!' he said when he came in. 'I needed that.' He stood over her, silhouetted against the brilliant sun. His sleek black hair was curling and drops of sea water glittered on his wide shoulders and lean torso like diamonds.

'I'm glad you enjoyed it.'

'Yes, you do allow me the brief moment,' he said. Expertly he twirled his large beach towel so it was arranged alongside, then he lowered

himself on to it, propping himself up on one
elbow as he gazed down on her beautiful, lightly
gilded body. Though very blonde she had the
most fortunate of skins. It never freckled and it
never, treated sensibly, ever burned. Her face she
only exposed to the sun briefly, but even then it
caught gold.

'Magic,' he murmured. 'Nature has been too
kind to you, Claudia.'

'*You* should talk.'

'A man's looks don't matter so much.'

'*Don't* they?' she said dryly. 'Yours have made
a lot of legs give out.'

'Aren't you going to sunbathe topless?'

'I've thought of it.'

'Then you must *do* it.' There was a faint
savagery in his mocking voice.

'No thank you.'

'Do you fear someone might come?'

'Actually,' she opened her eyes to look at him.
'My main fear is *you*.'

'Well you certainly know how to seduce. I'm
finding it unbelievably difficult not to lick all that
oil off you.'

They swam again, then they had lunch and all
the while Claudia knew he was holding himself in
abeyance. Where he was aggressive she turned
aside his mockery with a soft voice, offering him
the best of everything Fergy had packed for their
picnic lunch. Yet there were only flashes when he
responded and once an easy endearment that
must have slipped out.

It was a tantalising day. They went for a long
walk to a magnificent lion shaped rock while the
seagulls swirled over the tumbling breakers and

dived with shrieking cries for fish. She found some very pretty shells, so many she had to collect them in her towelling hat but then Nick observed that the sun was too strong and she would get burned. Only then did she murmur plaintively she didn't think he would care.

Excitement and tension burned steadily in her all the way home. Her skin was sheened with salt and she should have been feeling exquisitely relaxed.

'Thank you, Nick,' she sighed as they reached the city limits.

'I'm so glad you had a nice time.'

She laughed shakily. 'Didn't you?'

'It was just fine.' With his hair ruffled into crisp curls and his tan deepened he looked like a particularly handsome gypsy, so it was that much more of a shock when he turned his head and one was confronted by a pair of startling light eyes. It was enough to induce a crisis of the nerves.

'I could do with a shower,' she managed weakly, several miles on.

'And what's more, you're having it at *my* place.'

'Not a bit. I'm going home.'

'That's what *you* think, lady.'

At this point, inexplicably, she lost her temper. 'All right, Nick, you've been simmering all day.'

'Oh, good, you've noticed.'

'I've done everything I can to please you.'

'Then continue to. Just shut up until we get home.'

'Here we are again!' she said, as they entered the quiet house.

'It's okay if you have a shower first.'

'Thanks, I'll wait. It sounds as though you're planning to drown me.'

He gripped her hand and escorted her up the stairs. 'Come on now, I won't join you if that's what you're worried about.'

'Look it's only a bit of salt.'

He showed her where he kept the towels. 'Get a move on would you? I have something to say to you.'

It was impossible to relax her body or her brain. Neither did she have any underclothes she realised. She had worn her bikini beneath her cotton smock.

Nick's towelling robe was hanging behind the bathroom door. It was short so it would do nicely. She could rinse out her bikini and pop it in the dryer. As she expected sand had been forced into the lining. She couldn't attempt to wash her hair out. It was so thick it took ages even with a blowdryer.

She stepped beneath the strong, steaming spray trying to prepare some alibi for herself . . .

'Come on,' his brisk tap on the door urged her.

She wondered if she had gone off. Certainly she had been engrossed in thought. She dried herself swiftly with the large, fluffy blue towel, used Nick's comb on her hair then draped his yellow towelling robe around her slender figure, belting it tightly. Her smock she left over the rail and her bikini she wrapped in a hand towel, preparatory to taking it to the dryer.

'What in the world were you . . . doing?' He started off assertively and trailed off.

'Oh, I borrowed your robe.'

'I can see that. It stopped me in my tracks.'

'You don't mind? I hadn't planned on coming back here. I've only got . . .'

'Don't explain. As soon as I start to feel nasty you decide to look wonderful.'

She blinked and steered around him. 'May I put my swimsuit in the dryer? I want to wear it home.'

He groaned lightly and stood a minute with his eyes shut. 'Claudia Ingram, Goddess, Avenging Angel, Circe, what else?'

'*Idiot*. Better add that to your list.'

'Where to you think that kind of an apology will get you?'

'I'd better dry my swim suit, Nick,' she cried. She moved like a gazelle down the hallway and he laughed sharply and went to have his own shower.

Maybe she could get round him. Claudia decided to make them martinis. A very dry martini was one of her father's favourites so she knew how to make it. She could even cook dinner. Fergy had made sure she was pretty clever in the kitchen. She was so anxious she found she was talking to herself. 'Look, Nick, I've totally *changed*.'

It was indeed the case. For many long months now she had driven herself crazy. She had agonised over a relationship that hadn't even existed. Now the misery, the unrelenting desperation had been driven from her mind. Everything her grandfather had said was true. Far from being attracted to Cristina Nick had never displayed more than the smooth politeness required of him. He could never have brought himself to such a relationship. He had told her that right at the beginning but instead of accepting his word without question she had allowed a woman she didn't really know to poison her mind.

Well, she had paid for it. It had all but ruined her twenty-first birthday party. It had given her months of anger and anguish and resentment.

'What are you up to?' Nick's voice was casual, offhand. He had changed into white cotton slacks with an open neck soft shirt and his grey eyes had caught something of its aquamarine colour. In fact he gleamed with a kind of angry energy or excitement.

She picked up the two cocktail glasses and stood in front of him. 'An aperitif before dinner.'

'I don't need any aphrodisiacs.' His narrowed eyes mocked her.

'Oh, well, they might help us through a bad patch.'

'You've concluded that, have you?' He glanced around. 'Come and sit beside me on the sofa.'

Claudia settled herself with her legs under her, trying to look companionable when Nick's manner was far from reassuring.

'So dear Cristina is having a baby?' he said so crisply she withdrew into her corner.

'I'm hoping it will make a new woman out of her.'

He turned his head to stare at her. 'I take it you had some passing thought it might be mine?'

Her expression was a pent-up plea for forgiveness.

'What's up? Cat got your tongue? I said Cristina is having a bloody baby.'

'Which is naturally my father's.'

'Of course, though I expect your worries won't entirely disappear until that fact is clearly recognisable?'

She gulped on her drink and choked a little. 'I don't really like this, you know.'

'Too heavy on the gin.'

'*Is* it?' she asked in tones of amazement.

'Surely I will *kill* you,' he muttered.

'I'm sorry, Nick.' She set her fragile glass down rather too firmly and slid forward to rest her head on his shoulder. 'If I've ever doubted you for a minute, I've suffered for it.'

'*You've* suffered for it!' He wrenched himself away from her so violently, leaping up, she fell full length. 'You seem to think you can say, I'm sorry, Nick, and that's it. You seem to think you can accuse me, suspect me, of all manner of things, then when I look like taking off my shoe to you, you snuggle up to me like a child.'

'I don't see why not? It's as plain as the nose on my face I haven't grown up.'

'You even put my robe around you like protective armour.'

'Then *hate* me.' She was struggling to get up. 'You're a hundred times more good and brilliant than I deserve. I'm too easily shocked. I believe everything anyone tells me. Even a madwoman. I'm too young. I lack character and I'm scared. Scared of *you*, Nick.'

She was talking, moving so precipitously, she couldn't prevent herself from tripping over a gorgeous Aubusson rug.

'I *quit*!' she shouted and burst into tears.

'You don't want me, I see.' He picked her up

with a degree of violence. 'Do you think that's
going to break my heart?'

'*What* heart?' Now she was petrified his robe
might come off.

'Is the robe coming loose?' He sounded deeply
ironic. 'Oh, your beautiful breasts, Claudia. I've
been hard pressed to keep my hands off them
since you were sixteen.'

'You *managed*,' she cried.

'Oh, you little bitch.'

He tumbled them both on to the couch and her
head fell back against the rich pile of cushions.
She couldn't believe that Nick would hurt her.
On the other hand he might.

'You shouldn't lose your temper, Nick,' she
said fervently.

He got one arm under her and pulled her into
his iron grasp. 'That's a little big for you, isn't
it?' The robe had lots of room in it and now it
had fallen back exposing her naked breasts. He
bent his head forward and took a rosy peak into
his mouth.

'*Nick!*' she arched back.

'Why can't you *believe* in me?' He lifted his
head but his hand kept possession of her breast.

'What's the point of going on about that?'

'Ssssh!'

It was like a tremendous fall in slow motion.
She thought she would never stop spiralling. He
lifted his mouth and began to stroke her. 'You
have no notion of how much I love you,' he said.

'You *won't* hate me, will you?' She quickened
and trembled and covered his face with little,
panting kisses. 'I will never let anyone *lie* to me
anymore.'

'Okay. Then it's all over. I want to keep you here forever.'

'Oh, God, *yes*,' she breathed. Her pulses were beating crazily, her long slender legs were free of the robe that crossed above her knees. 'I love you. *Love* you,' her voice was a little wild.

'Aaah!' He buried his head between her breasts. 'What can we do really? I'll do anything you ask.'

'Then love me,' she half whispered. 'I don't want to wait.'

'You can't be *certain* of that, my darling.' His voice was so gentle it brought tears to her eyes. 'What about the day you're my bride? My young, radiant, excited bride. I want everything to be perfect for you. No sense of sadness, or regret.'

'But I want you so desperately, Nick,' she faltered. 'How can you be so cruel?'

'Cruel, oh my God!' He twisted her head back and kissed her drowningly and as he held her in his arms she could feel the trembling in his body. In love, he was incredibly unselfish. Though the fire of passion consumed them now, there was something exultant in coming to him as a virgin bride.

She knew now he loved her deeply. She truly knew it. When she opened her eyes to him they were sweet pools of enchantment. 'I don't want a quiet wedding. I want a *big* one. I want everyone in the world to know how I'm *blessed*.'

'And what's more, you want it at Easter,' he said masterfully. 'Easter comes early this year.'

She sighed voluptuously and moved Nick's robe back up on her shoulders. 'I'd give the whole world for you, do you know that?'

Joy had given her a lustre that took his breath away.

With the air of a man who was tested to the limit, he forced himself to his feet, drawing her up with him and holding her within his encircling arms.

'Sir Galahad couldn't hold a candle to me in my opinion.'

'No,' she breathed smilingly. She let her head fall forward against his breast. 'But *after* the wedding you have my permission to be *yourself*.'

Grant and Cristina Ingram's baby was delivered by Caesarian section in the first week of August. A perfectly formed boy who even in his newness was the image of his father. Mother and father were ecstatic with pride and joy.

Nick and Claudia were in London at the time and Nick took his father-in-law's jubilant telephone call at two o'clock in the morning.

'I thought you would want to know right away!' Grant Ingram called over the wires.

Nick expressed his sincere pleasure and passed the phone to his waiting wife. Claudia took it staring up into his brilliant eyes. They had enjoyed a marvellous evening and had only arrived back at their hotel a few minutes before.

All the time Claudia was talking to her father, Nick was kissing her neck and bare shoulders. She melted against him while he released the zipper on her low-backed jade chiffon dress.

She was trembling as she replaced the receiver. 'They're both well. Isn't that marvellous?'

'*Marvellous!*' Nick burst out laughing. 'That Cristina really throws herself into the part, doesn't she? My God, what an actress she would have made!'

Cristina from the very day she had discovered she was pregnant had virtually become an amnesiac, blanking out every episode in her life she wished to forget.

Very slowly Nick continued to undress his young wife, inhaling her soft scent, then when the excitement became too strong for them, he carried her to the bed. All else now was too far away, too inconsequential . . .

Claudia lifted her slender arms and pulled him down to heaven.

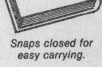